Wilted Minds

Stories of Sex, Addiction and Lost Love

A Novel by Elliot M. Rubin

Wilted Minds

Stories of Sex, Addiction and Lost Love

First edition

Library of Congress
ISBN # 978-0-9913060-6-0

Acknowledgements

I would like to thank my late father, Herman S. Rubin, for his inspiration to write.

He wrote essays, prayers, and poetry his whole life and his writings are treasured by those who have read them.

And lastly, and most importantly, I want to continue to thank my dear wife Laura, whom I love very much, for her keen disinterest that kept driving me to write more.

Chapter One – The Beginning

As Barbara trudged slowly walked uphill onto the pathway to the George Washington Bridge she was breathing very heavily. Her lungs were straining to take in air. Her enormous morbidly obese body was causing her to stop every few feet to catch her breath, as her heart was pounding and trying to burst out of her chest.

Slowly sweat was dripping down her forehead and also running from her armpits down the sides of her blouse. It was excruciatingly painful with every small step she took. But she was determined to get to the middle of the bridge, ignoring the many signs and call boxes for the suicide help lines.

This spring day was very beautiful with the sun softly beating down on her and a gentle cooling breeze blowing on her cherubic face; while chilling the sweat on her many chins and on her corpulent body.

Manhattan was directly ahead of her as she finally started to walk on the pedestrian path of the bridge at a snail's pace. Every few feet she had to stop, hold onto the railing for support, and catch her breath.

There were other pedestrians alongside of her and a few cyclists on the walkway that day also; they were enjoying the sun and placid gusts of wind that blew by them with the scent of the river rising up, yet the water was hurdling at a frantic pace below.

When she finally reached the center of the span, exhausted, she stopped and looked over the edge.

It was a steep drop.

Barbara put both of her hands on the cold gray steel railing and started to look around. The small gold cross that she wore around her neck glistened in the warm sunlight while resting on her heaving massive breasts as she gasped for air.

As she stood there gazing out, to her left was the skyline of New York City with the rush of morning traffic at her back whizzing past on their way to the city.

On her right she saw the sheer cliffs of the New Jersey Palisades jutting out of the water, reaching for the clouds. The forest of apartment houses on both sides of the Hudson River seemed so small and far away at that moment.

People were ignoring her as they were walking intently past her back. She stared, transfixed, downriver from the bridge towards the New York Harbor in the distance. The tumbling waves below the bridge, with their little white caps, mesmerized her as she continued to look at them. She did not move; she just kept staring at the water from above. She ignored the people behind her as they too did not even notice her standing there. She was invisible to everyone, yet she was hard to miss due to her size.

Her feelings were not paining her as they did in the past. By now she was numb from the emotional hurt that had followed her throughout her existence.

A feeling that the burden of life was suddenly lifted off her shoulders overcame her. Finally, she felt mentally relieved.

Barbara took in a deep breath of the cold river air that was blowing so high up, and it filled her lungs. A very slight chill ran through her body at that moment. Her thin cotton floral blouse fluttered in the breeze, not offering her any protection from the lightly chilled wind.

The railing was about four feet high or so and it presented a major problem to her. She was not sure if she could raise her enormously heavy legs and thighs over the railing.

Maybe…Barbara thought, that if she stood up on her toes, she might be able to just pull herself up and slide over it and go head first into the river.

Maybe….

"I wonder if it will hurt" she said to herself as she stood there. She had read about other people jumping off the bridge to end it all. The New York Post even showed where on the bridge the last jumper leapt from. But they never said anything about it hurting, or people surviving. It has to be better than jumping in front of a subway train, she thought. Who wants to be smashed into a moving train? She knew that definitely would hurt.

This was not going to be a planned out in detail type of jump. It was a spur of the moment kind of thing that she thought of when her heart was broken, a quick decision and a solution to a problem. Not that she had second thoughts about doing it, just how to do it.

The hurt from the breakup and the humiliation she endured was too much for her to overcome. She was left alone with nobody in the world that would even care if she was alive or dead, or even miss her.

"Maybe this was not such a good idea after all", she began to think to herself as she realized the railing was a bit too high for her. She began to have second thoughts on her swan dive into oblivion.

Cars started to screech to a halt behind her. She thought that maybe there was an accident because she heard a lot of car horns blowing and people shouting. But their voices were muffled due to the wind and she could not make out what they were saying.

Holding on to the railing she slowly turned around and saw a car stopped on the roadway directly behind where she was standing.

A man in a business suit hurriedly jumped out of the driver's side door. He started running around the front of his car and easily hurdled over the inner guardrail and landed on the walkway, tumbling right in front of where she was standing, only a few feet away from her.

He stood up to catch his breath and steady his feet, and looked directly at her. He was motionless for a moment and stared at her, but said nothing. He waited one second to get his bearings, and then backed up a foot or so and then started running again. This time he ran right towards the railing next to where Barbara was standing.

Barbara did not know what he was going to do. Caught completely off guard and frozen with fear she saw him coming towards her at full speed and she closed her eyes, fearing an impact when he hit her. He was only about five feet away from her when he stated to run.

He veered off to the right, next to her, and grabbed the guard rail with both of his hands. He jumped up and swung his legs over the outer walkway railing and went over. In one quick smooth motion like a high jumper would do at a track meet he vaulted over the railing towards the river; flailing his arms and legs in the air as he plunged towards his death.

Barbara heard him next to her as he hurled himself into the river and she turned to follow his fall. She stood there watching his descent as if it were in slow motion.

She saw him go down until he landed in the river with a silent splatter. He went below the water line and disappeared down into the dark murky river. She had followed his descent into the river with her eyes transfixed. Straining to hear, she tried to listen for a splashing sound when she saw the plume of water rise into the air from where he entered, but heard nothing.

Just like that it was over.

He made no sounds, no screams, not even a whimper that she could discern.

Stunned by what she just witnessed, Barbara did not move. She had never seen anyone kill themselves before; especially directly in front of her.

Her thoughts of suicide at that moment were gone in a flash as Port Authority Police came running towards her. Surrounded by police, she stood still, frozen with disbelief at what she had just witnessed.

The police hurriedly asked her if he said anything to her before he jumped over the railing. Or did he leave a note, or a package, or anything so that they might have some motive or leads.

She told them he quietly just ran by her and jumped over the railing. Another police officer calmly called in for a police boat to try and find the body. The police did not seem that concerned with the jumper. They knew he was dead and it was a fifty/fifty chance they would find his body before it floated out to sea and be eaten by the fish.

He had left nothing but his car running on the bridge, blocking traffic.

As the police started questioning her, a car with some inner city young men was slowly driving by the man's stopped car. Their car slowed down and then stopped for a split second as it pulled even with the dead man's vehicle. One of the boys jumped out, got behind the steering wheel of the idling car and then floored the gas pedal and peeled out; driving it away into the bowels of upper Manhattan.

Barbara and the police just stood there in disbelief at the car theft that just happened right in front of them. The police were in such a hurry to find witnesses on the walkway that they didn't even have time to write his license plate number down to try and identify him later. They never expected someone to steal a car on the top of the bridge. He was an unknown jumper, another number for their files.

The traffic on the bridge started to pick up again as there was nothing blocking them anymore; until a police van came to where they were standing and stopped traffic again.

The police wanted to question her some more and they asked her if she would accompany them to their station for a few minutes. Barbara felt she had no choice in the matter and she agreed to go with them. She was very slowly escorted off the bridge by two Port Authority officers.

She could not walk very fast and they held her arms on each side as they carefully and sluggishly walked her to the end of the walkway in New Jersey. Then they all went down the stairs at the beginning of the bridge holding onto the railing for support.

Waiting for them at the small parking space was a Port Authority vehicle for them to enter. The three of them left the bridge walkway and sat down in the Authority van.

Cautiously they helped her get into the passenger seat in the front of the van. She was too big to get in the rear door and slide over. They also had trouble buckling the seatbelt around her so she just sat there, exhausted from all the walking. Her stomach almost touched the dashboard as she slumped on to the passenger seat.

Carefully they drove Barbara in the small passenger van to their office in New Jersey to question her a second time in more detail; and record some personal information about her since she was the only close witness. They had to bring her in because she told them she could not stand on the bridge any longer answering questions. Her tree trunk legs were starting to give out. She had never planned to walk back down to the stairway and standing there was just too much strain on her body.

When they finally arrived at the building they retrieved a wheel chair to get her inside. But it was a tight fit and she had to squeeze into the chair and sit sideways to actually sit down into it.

A large officer who worked out every day volunteered to push the wheelchair into the building; it was so heavy from her weight.

Once she was inside the building they brought her into a small interview room where they would be questioning her in detail on what she had seen.

She was asked to be seated at a wooden table in the center of the room with a few small ladder back chairs around it.

The police captain, a veteran of over twenty five years on the force, slowly walked into the room where she was sitting and stood still in the doorway for a moment. He stared at her not believing how large she was. Finally he casually walked over to the middle of the room and sat down opposite her at the table. He cupped his hands in front of him and calmly asked her why she was on the bridge that day. Did she walk there often, he asked.

He was exceptionally suspicious as it was very unusual for an extremely overweight woman to walk half the length of the bridge by herself just to look at the scenery.

The captain knew that she had to leave her car in the park on the Jersey side. Then she would have had to climb a large steep stairway leading to the bridge, and someone in her shape would only do that if they were extremely motivated. The question he wanted an answer to was why? But he had his misgivings as to the answer she might give him.

He knew it was not unusual for someone to commit suicide from the top of the bridge.

She told the captain her full name and where she lived. Barbara also told him she had driven to the park at the foot of the bridge in Fort Lee New Jersey and walked up to the stairway. That she also had left her pocket book in her car, unlocked. Barbara said she hid her keys under the rear floor mat so no one would steal her car.

This certainly did not make sense to the captain. If anything it just confirmed his suspicions as to why she was there in the first place.

Barbara had no intention of going back to the car so she did not care if it was locked or not. But surprisingly she did not want it stolen. Her thoughts were not very clear that day.

But she did not answer his question as to why she was on the bridge that day, and he knew she was hedging her answer.

"Barbara" the captain said very softly, "I don't think you came here today to walk on the bridge just to see the sights. Why did you really come here today?"

"Does it matter?" she replied softly, looking away from him at the wall behind him.

"To me it does" he tried to answer in a caring manner. Then he waited, silently, for his answer. The silence at that moment was unnerving. Neither said anything but sat there silently, waiting for the other to say something else. He wanted an answer and she did not want to give one.

Barbara turned her head and looked around the room at the faded blue paint on the office walls. It was not peeling but she could tell it had been years since it was painted.

There was that small table that she was sitting at and a few small very solid wooden chairs around it, and not much else. The chair was really not big enough to accommodate her and Barbara's rear end hung over on both sides of the hard wooden seat. She started to squirm a little trying to get comfortable but it didn't help. The chairs were purposefully bought to be uncomfortable and to make the people sitting in them want to leave. All they had to do was answer the questions posed to them and then they thought they could go.

She was a little nervous being in that room. Without any forewarning she felt that the walls were closing in on her and she broke out in a steady flow of sweat. Her breathing got heavier and she started to sweat more profusely.

Her windblown medium length dirty blond hair was starting to stick to her forehead from the moisture on her brow. From under her triple chins the downward flow of sweat started to stain the top of her thin flowery blouse.

She felt that the room was getting warmer. Even though she was a very heavy set woman she usually took great personal care of herself. But that morning she felt very depressed and didn't shower or use her under arm antiperspirant.

The beads of perspiration started to drip down her body from her arm pits and become a steady stream of warm fluid. She felt the wet liquid slide between her arms and her rib cage. And it started to come from underneath her braless breasts and down her rib cage to her waist and then roll over to the side of her body.

The captain was sitting across the table from her and noticed her physical discomfort. He noticed that she was ever so slightly starting to squirm in the chair from nerves.

The front of her blouse was now fully wet and stained and clinging to her from her perspiration. The nipples of her breasts were now protruding through the thoroughly soaked shirt. At that point the captain now felt uncomfortable being in the room with her alone and pressed the intercom and asked for a policewoman to come into the room with them.

"Would you like a cold cup of water?" he asked her.

"Yes, thank you" she responded. "Could you open a window or something" she continued, "It is getting very hot in here."

But there were no windows in that interrogation room.

As the policewoman opened the door and entered the room to sit with them, the captain got up to get Barbara some water. At the moment he stood up Barbara put her hands on the table, placed her left foot out to the side from in front of the chair and started to roll her eyes backwards into her head.

"Captain!" the policewoman yelled at him as he was leaving the room and closing the door behind him. He turned and saw Barbara slowly slump over and hit her head on the table as she fell to the floor with a soft yet powerful thud.

She was bleeding from a soft tissue gash on her head. The blood was gushing out and forming a small red pool on the floor. Barbara's eyes closed and she passed out as she turned onto her back. Her body went limp and her legs flailed out from under her hitting the table leg. The heavy wooden table shook and moved slightly from the sheer weight of her enormous legs. The policewoman quickly jumped up from her seat and ran out of the room to get the emergency first aid kit. When she rushed back in she put on latex gloves, and called for an ambulance.

The female officer knelt down by Barbara and placed two gauze pads together over the wound on her head, applying pressure to stem the blood flow.

This incident happened in the morning. By dinner time Barbara awoke and found out she was in a hospital emergency room in Bergen County. She had an IV drip in her arm and a hospital security guard sitting just outside the curtain where they placed her.

Barbra's wet clothes were cut off of her and two washed out pale blue hospital gowns were placed on her to cover her up, with a thin white sheet placed over her body to give her more privacy.

A petite nurse walked in to check up on her and patted her on her hand; she reassured her that everything will be okay. She told Barbara she had fainted at the police station, cut her head open on a table when she fell, and was brought here for stitches and to recover. She also had contusions on her legs that were turning black and blue from when she had kicked the wooden table in the interrogation room.

"Am I under arrest?" Barbara asked the nurse.

"I am not really sure" she answered back. "But there is a security guard sitting on the other side of the curtain. I will go and check your chart. If you are, there should be a notation about that" the nurse told her, as she turned and left the cubicle.

It really didn't matter if she was or not. Without clothes, shoes or a car she was not going anywhere anyway.

The minutes seemed like hours to Barbara as she laid on the hospital gurney. Thirty minutes later a doctor in a white hospital jacket came in to her cubicle to speak to her, holding an open manila folder.

"Hi Barbara, how are you feeling?" he asked in a soothing masculine tone.

"My head hurts a lot" she responded.

"Yes, I think it would. You had to have a few stitches on your head where you fell. In a day or two you will be feeling a lot better. I can order you a light pain pill if you like, to take the edge off" he asked her.

"No, it's not that bad, thanks" she answered him. "I'm used to pain" she told him.

What he didn't know was that she found pain a sexual turn on. But he would find that out at a later time.

"Barbara, my name is Doctor Willentz" he introduced himself to her. "I am a psychiatrist. I want to ask you a question Barbara. Were you on the bridge today because you wanted to hurt yourself?"

Mental health professionals are trained to get to the point and not beat around the bush. This usually takes a person off guard as society teaches us to be restrained in our questions. The answers are usually honest and forthcoming, but not always.

"No. I had no plans to jump over the side. I just felt like I had to be there, in the middle of the river. I was feeling a little down today. That's all" she told him.

But he could tell that was not the whole truth. She hesitated as she spoke to him.

"Barbara" he continued, "I believe... that you were not there to admire the view" he told her.

The fact that she mentioned she was not there to jump over the side was the answer he was looking for. He knew that was not a truthful answer.

She started to cry. Finally she admitted that she was depressed. But that was as far as she was going to admit to him.

"I am going to keep you here for a few days under psychiatric observation; and we can talk a little more tomorrow when you are feeling better" Doctor Willentz told her.

He smiled at her and turned to walk out of the room when she called out to him "I'm not crazy, just tired and confused".

He stopped at the door, turned to her and said in a confident manner "I know, I am here to help you and I want you to know that."

After he left an orderly came in and asked if she would like something to eat. The food cart was coming around and she wanted to see if Barbara was hungry.

It was now seven in the evening and the last time she ate was very early in the morning, about 5 am when she awoke.

At home that morning she had made two stacks of real buttermilk pancakes, smothered in genuine Vermont maple syrup poured over the buttered pancakes. After the pancakes she had half of a delicious all chocolate layer cake she had bought at the supermarket with a quart of very cold whole milk to wash it down. Dietetic foods were not to be found in her home.

By now she was hungry again. She hadn't eaten in almost twenty four hours. When she left her home in the morning she didn't think she would have to worry about lunch or dinner ever again.

"Yes, please, if it is not too much trouble" she answered.

The orderly brought her a tray with a white meat covered with yellow gravy. She was told it was turkey. The green beans on the side of the tray were wrinkled and dry looking. She took the butter that came with her small roll and tried to place it over the green beans to give them some taste. But the green beans were coldish and the butter did not melt. That did not stop her, she ate everything anyway.

Between the IV drip and the small meal she was now somewhat full and not too hungry.

In the next hour or so a young male orderly with a short goatee and wearing a hospital uniform came in to her room. Barbara had not noticed him before in the emergency room but that did not matter. He asked her if she would like a sponge bath to freshen up a little. He explained to Barbara that the head nurse suggested it as she noticed that "your clothes were stained from sweat and you might enjoy it as it is very relaxing" he told her. "But if you would like a female orderly I can get one, but she doesn't come on duty till the next shift tonight" he told her.

"No," Barbara said. "You can do it. I don't care".

It had been a short while since a man had touched her and she was not hesitant at all. She closed her eyes and just waited for him to begin washing her down. In her mind he looked greasy and a low life but she was too tired to care. Anyway, there were too many men who had been touching her while she was at work, and this would just be one more.

With her positive answer he took out a bowl of warm water and two wash cloths, and soaked them in the bowl. He wringed one out and gently washed Barbara's face with it.

The coolness of the water on her face took the tenseness out of her body. She took a deep breath and her body slumped down on the hard hospital bed and into a relaxed, almost floating position. Her arms went limp and she just waited for the sponge bath to begin.

The orderly proceeded to sponge bathe her whole body until the odor of sweat left the room. Lifting her heavy legs was not easy but he was able to do it. He bent one leg and gently slid the mildly wet wash cloth over her skin. Then he lowered it and bent the other leg and did the same thing.

Barbara began to enjoy it. He slowly washed her upper inner thighs and stopping just before he reached her genital area. The anticipation of his hands almost touching her there began to excite her.

She began to enjoy the gentleness of his hands as he washed her body carefully. First dampening the skin, then with a little soap slowly caressing her from head to foot, he washed her whole immense body in this manner. She started to get a stirring in her lower abdomen that she did not have for a while now; especially when he gently lifted her breasts to wash under them as he had also washed her inner thighs. A rush swept through her body from her thighs to her arms. She began to get light headed from the thrill of his touching her. She closed her eyes and laid there enjoying every moment of his washing her, wanting more.

Refreshed when it was over Barbara thanked the nurse and started to close her eyes, hoping that he would come back tomorrow and do it again.

The night nurse then walked in and gave her a sleeping pill which she took with a small cup of water.

Her dinner tray was removed and she closed her eyes and drifted off until the next morning.

Early the next day an orderly came to move her bed, with her in it. Barbara was wheeled through the hallways of the hospital until they reached the elevator that was in the rear of the wing. She was brought upstairs to a secure psychiatric floor and a bigger gown was found for her. But they had to use two bath robes to cover her up.

Once she was brought into her room they had a hard time moving her to a better bed in the room. It took four nurses to shift her out of the emergency room bed onto theirs. Doctor Willentz came in to see her after she was in the new bed. He asked her if she was comfortable in the bed and if she needed anything else while she was there.

"Tomorrow I would like to move you to my institute in North Jersey where we can do more talking. It is much nicer than the hospital to stay in. Do you have any objections to that?" He asked.

"No, I guess that will be okay" she responded in a low quiet voice.

He continued "I have a grant from a hospital research foundation that wants to test intensive group therapy in a one week period instead of just an hour a day as is usually done. That way we can try to get you back on your feet emotionally and on your way to a better life much quicker. It will be at no cost to you. Any questions?" he asked.

She shook her head from side to side.

"Okay, then tomorrow I will have the transfer done. See you in the morning." he told her.

Barbara looked to the left and peered out the window of her room. She wondered how high up she was and if the window opened. Then she noticed the steel bars on the window and she immediately realized they were solid glass windows and do not open.

Resigned to the reality of her situation she decided to watch the small television by her bed. She put on the television and started to watch a game show.

At home she usually watched the news and got depressed whenever something happened to a small child. Either maimed or killed, it upset her greatly and brought back memories she had tried for so long to repress. She would then change the channel to something more light hearted and mindless.

She heard the soft rumble of the food cart outside her room stop and the trays bounce ever so slightly. A breakfast tray was brought in for her and placed on a table by her bedside. When the cover was removed she saw French toast, syrup, some strawberries, and a container of iced tea. In that psyche ward they do not bring metal knives and forks, even plastic ones. She had a combo spoon and fork to eat with.

She sat up, pulled the moveable table over to her bed, placed it over her legs, and started to eat her breakfast.

The food was portion controlled and she was still hungry when she had finished eating. So she took the phone and called down to the kitchen and requested another breakfast be brought up to her. In forty minutes an orderly came into her room and brought her a second breakfast. She lifted the plastic cover and saw they had brought her scrambled eggs, toast and potatoes and coffee. She smiled and started to eat it all.

When she finished breakfast she sat there silently. Her thoughts were on tomorrow when she would be transferred out of there.

The rest of the day was boring and dragged on. She was getting slightly agitated and cranky from boredom, due to doing nothing. So the nurses sedated her again and she fell asleep.

When the ambulance crew came for her the next day they had to get extra help to slide her onto the gurney and wheel her down the hall to the elevator. Once outside they opened the rear door and placed her in the ambulance. Then they drove off to the institute taking the Palisades Parkway north.

The ride was a little over a half hour or so.

Once she was admitted in and assigned a room she was placed in a wheel chair and brought upstairs. The floor nurse told her that Doctor Willentz and his assistant would be coming in to see her shortly and to just relax and take it easy.

When he finally did walk in he asked how she was feeling and said that tomorrow they would start the group sessions. She would be getting new scrubs and a bathrobe that fit her and slippers also. Her clothes were cut off in the hospital emergency room and discarded, but they did have her pocket book put away for safe keeping.

Chapter Two - Mei 메이

A young nurse walked into Barbara's room to get her and escort her down the hall for the first day's group therapy session. They walked slowly and then turned to the right, into a midsized room with seven chairs arranged in a semi-circle.

Doctor Willentz was sitting in the middle chair and five other people were sitting there with him waiting for Barbara to enter the room. They were a mixed bunch of people, one man, four women, and everyone except Doctor Willentz was in hospital scrubs.

"Good morning Barbara" Doctor Willentz greeted her as she entered the room. "We are starting a new group session today for one week and everyone here is new to this. Each of you will get a chance to speak and ask questions. But I am asking that you introduce yourselves by your first name only. When I ask a question each of you will get a chance to respond if you wish.

"We will be here together for one week and hopefully we can resolve some issues that you might be having. Everything you say here is privileged and cannot be repeated by anyone. Even in a court of law" Doctor Willentz continued.

"Please introduce yourselves so we all know who we are talking too" he told everyone.

"We can start on my left".

"My name is Jose."

"My name is Dawn."

"My name is Shaniqua."

"My name is Amanda."

"My name is Barbara."

"My name is Mei, M.E.I. but it is pronounced May. I am Korean."

"Thank you and we can start with Mei; please tell us something about yourself." Doctor Willentz said to her.

"I was born in South Korea. I am twenty five years old and have been living here since I was five" she said in a soft voice. "My parents came here on a work visa and I came to America with them."

"When I was seven my father was killed in a car accident while going to work. The boss arranged for a van to take him to a Korean restaurant he owned in Queens to work as a cook; when the van he was in was hit by a big truck. He was killed instantly and the van driver had no insurance. My mother and I were very poor and had nothing to live on."

"Not having any highly trained work skills my mother had a hard time taking care of the both of us. She took jobs cleaning many people's homes and apartments for whatever money they would pay her."

"Soon after my father died my mother's family in Korea forced her to marry a much older Korean man named Young-soo, who lived here in America. They had arranged it from overseas and told her that Young-soo would take care of her and me. It is considered a family disgrace in Korea to be a single mother, even though she was in America and a widow. My mother still had the old country values in her."

She continued "Young-soo was a butcher in a Korean meat market in Queens and he was about thirty years older than my mother. He also had saved all his money as he never was married or spent his money on anything. He would go home to his apartment, turn on a Korean television station, and drink beer while he watched the Korean television shows on cable."

"His apartment had very old used furniture with the stuffing coming out of the sofa. He had no taste or style. And he only shaved once a week, after his shower!"

"No one else would marry him, he was so ugly. But he had the wealth to care for us. My mother was depressed and desperate and he was introduced to her by a matchmaker her family had hired. Everyone thought it was for the best for both of them."

"When he was sober he was kind and thoughtful to us. But when he drank too much he would beat my mother. I was a little girl and I often witnessed this. But that was not too bad physically for me, until I reached eleven years old. Then one night when he was drunk he looked at me funny for the first time, but I did not realize what he was going to do."

"My mother always went to bed around nine o'clock. She had to get up early to get to work in Manhattan for her job cleaning hotel rooms. Meanwhile Young-soo sat on the sofa and continued drinking beer and watching television. He would get up the next day whenever he awoke, and then he would open his shop. His prices were very low, and anyway the neighborhood people knew that he was always late opening the store so they never came to him very early."

"That night when he was sure my mother was sleeping he quietly came into my room. He lifted my blanket off of me and stood there and looked down at me. I opened my eyes and saw him standing there. I said nothing, I was frozen with fear. Slowly, and softly, he put his hand under my nightgown and placed it on my leg. He started to rub it softly, up and down. He slid his hand between my thighs and I started to really wake up. I felt him gently rub my pubic hair. I was now awake and he placed his hand over my mouth and kept rubbing me."

"If you say anything" he whispered to me in Korean as he got close to my face, "or make any sounds I will beat you like I beat your mother."

"I could smell the alcohol on his breath as he started to breathe heavily. He bent down really close to my face and it was only inches away from my lips. He lifted my back upwards into a sitting position with his left arm and completely took off my nightgown. I was now fully awake but frozen and afraid to move. Then he started to kiss my tiny breasts and lick them. I didn't say anything and let him continue out of fear he would kill me."

"Slowly he moved his head downward towards my thighs, licking and kissing my skin. When he finally reached between my legs his tongue darted in and out and up and down. I was aroused for the first time in my life. I could not control my body. It seemed to move without my controlling it. I felt an urge that I never felt before. "

"I was feeling all wet down there and he took his finger and inserted it into me. I felt a twinge of pain as he started to move his finger more forcefully." Mei stopped speaking for a moment... then continued "and I was very excited."

"He unbuckled his pants and they dropped to the floor; and then he spun me around and lifted my legs straight up into the air and he had sex with me" Mei continued. "Once, twice and then when he was finished he reminded me that if I said anything he would punish me and my mother."

"I was only eleven years old and I did not know what to do. I feared he would beat me like he did my mother. Sometimes he took a frying pan and hit her very hard on the chest or arms. Twice she had to go to the hospital with broken bones in her arms and bruises on her chest. I dared not say anything to my mother about my sex with him or I really believed he would kill the both of us."

"How long did this go on" Doctor Willentz asked, interrupting her.

Mei didn't answer directly but continued her story.

"Then he started to sexually abuse me when my mom was working or was not home yet. And this went on almost every night until I turned thirteen. Then I ended it" Mei responded.

Shaniqua interrupted her and asked "how were you able to stop it being so young? Did you go to the police? Did you tell your mom?" she said to Mei.

"No. I did not report him. No one would believe me. Plus I was a young girl and I was afraid. It wasn't until I turned thirteen that I had the courage and took my revenge" Mei told her.

"There was this senior high school boy who hung out near my middle school, his name was Tommy O'Brian. I really had a big crush on him. For a white boy I thought he was very handsome, with long wavy brown hair and he wore tight fitting jeans. He was on one of the high school's sports teams and was very muscular too."

"One day I was hanging out on the sidewalk outside of middle school with my girlfriends and he noticed me. He walked over to us and started to talk to me. Jokingly he said to me that we should run away together, but I thought he was serious. Being young and immature I was not worldly then. I thought we would be together forever. I immediately had a school girl crush on him."

"So when I went to home to my apartment that afternoon after school I packed some underwear, my training bra and one blouse into a paper bag. In my mind I was going to run away with him the next day; and leave the sexual abuse behind. But before I did that I felt I first had to protect my mother from my stepfather. I was afraid he would kill her if I left and he had no one to abuse."

"That night I waited until my mother was asleep and he had finished drinking his many cans of beer. He leaned back on the sofa and fell into a deep sleep watching television, as usual. The volume was always very loud as I think he was hard of hearing. I waited till I heard him snoring then I quietly walked through the living room, past him sleeping on the sofa, and into the kitchen. I opened the kitchen drawer where all the knives were kept. I took out the largest meat cleaver I could find that he kept in the kitchen. He had a lot of knives in the house also."

"Since he was a butcher he often would bring a big piece of meat home for us. He would carve it up for my mother to freeze or cook to for dinner. So I opened the drawer and picked up the biggest meat cleaver I could lift. I then quietly walked behind the sofa where he was sleeping. It was very heavy and I had to use both hands to hold it."

"His head was tilted back on the sofa and his neck was exposed. The snoring was very loud, like a train or a truck coming through my living room. It was so loud it actually hurt my ears. I stood to the right, just behind him, and raised my arms as high as I could. It was not easy to lift it as the meat cleaver was really very heavy; and I was a tiny, thin, scrawny little girl."

"With one forceful motion, and all of my thirteen year old strength, I lowered the cleaver right into the middle of his throat. It landed right below his chin, on his neck. I heard the bones snap in his neck as I almost cut his head clear off of him. He never knew what hit him. Blood started to spurt out onto the floor."

"I heard some gurgling sounds coming from his throat as the escaping air from his lungs mixed with the blood pouring down his windpipe into his air way."

"The metal cleaver was very big and heavy. It did what it was supposed to do. Only the skin in the back of his neck kept his head from rolling down onto the floor behind the sofa. It just hung there, hanging by some muscle, as it rolled off of his shoulder. His eyes had snapped open and his arms flung wildly as his body tumbled to the floor, convulsing in spasms. Then he stopped moving."

"I dropped the cleaver onto the sofa next to where his body was laying and ran to the kitchen to wash some blood off my hands. Then I grabbed my paper bag, left a note for my mother telling her what he had been doing sexually to me when she was not home."

"I then ran out of the house to hide momentarily in the basement until the morning. That was my plan. But I was nervous and left the apartment house in the early morning when it was still dark out."

"My thoughts were to meet Tommy before he went to school and the both of us could run away together. The only drawback in that thinking was that Tommy did not have the same plans as I did. I was a kid, only thirteen, and didn't think things through."

"I walked along the streets of my neighborhood until dawn, waiting on the corner by his apartment building to meet up with Tommy. It was very quiet and there was nobody out walking except me."

"I heard the police sirens a few blocks away as they came to my apartment house in the morning. My mother had to have found him. I left a note for her telling her what he had done to me for all those years" as Mei repeated herself to the group.

"When Tommy did finally come out, he saw me and walked over to me. As I stood on the sidewalk looking at him my heart was racing; I was so excited to see him. I told him I was ready to run away with him. I didn't want to go back home anymore… and we could be together."

"He looked at me strangely and asked me what made me think he would do such a thing. I was only thirteen and really had no valid reason why. It was just my young heart imagining it. I guess maybe I was watching too many soap operas."

"I told him I could not go home as I did something very bad to my stepfather because he was raping me. After I said that Tommy looked at me and stood there for moment thinking. Then he took my hand in his and he walked back to his apartment with me following him. I think he then realized I was not a virgin and he could have some fun with me."

"Tommy unlocked the door and we walked into his place. His parents were at work by then and the apartment was empty except for us. He led me into his bedroom and he kept the light off. He turned to me and said he loved me. But today I know he was just lying to me to get into my pants. When I had told him earlier I had been raped by my stepfather and was not a virgin his face had changed; and he looked at me kind of differently. We now both sat down together on the edge of his bed and he turned to me, put his arms around me, and started to kiss me."

"The next thing I knew my blouse was unbuttoned and his hand was up my skirt. I didn't say anything as I was just happy to be with him. To be wanted and loved. He pushed me back onto the bed and swiftly pulled my underpants down. There was no foreplay to speak of, except for his licking my tiny breasts."

"He stood up and undressed quickly kicking off his sneakers and dropping his pants onto the floor."

"He took out some Vaseline and put it on his dick, and then he placed a pillow under me and lifted my legs high into the air. He started plunging into me, multiple times getting faster and faster. I was not excited at all when he started to screw me but I couldn't care; and I did not resist him. We had sex that morning a few times. I thought I loved him, he was so handsome."

"When he was finished I walked into his bathroom to clean up; he didn't use any condoms and I was a mess down there from him. Then we went into his living room naked and we both watched television together for a while. He liked to watch the morning game shows, so I sat next to him and watched them also."

"His apartment was kind of nice. It was clean and had a lot of gold velvet furniture with plastic slipcovers on all the sofas and chairs. When I sat on the sofa the plastic slip cover stuck to my ass and it felt funny when I stood up. There was red carpet all over the place and it was very soft to walk on, my feet sank into it. We didn't have any carpets at home; we had wood floors in our apartment. They were hard on my feet and we never wore shoes at home. That's an Asian custom."

"When it was lunch time Tommy said he had to go to school for a big test he had to take in the afternoon. Then we both got dressed and we walked out of his apartment. I stood behind him as he locked the door and we took the back stairway down to the lobby."

"I sat on the front steps outside his building and I watched him walk down the block and turn the corner. I was in love for the first time and had given myself to him freely. I really had a good time that morning with him."

"I didn't know that he didn't have a test that afternoon, but that he went to have lunch with his friends in school to brag that he screwed me. I found out about it after three o'clock when school let out and he came back with two of his buddies."

"Tommy kissed me when he saw me and took me by my hand and we went up to his place again with his two friends. I didn't know them or what was going on, he never introduced them to me. I just thought we were all going to watch television together and hang out a while."

"When we walked into his living room he spun me around and kissed me with his tongue going into my mouth. I never had that before and I was a little startled. He asked me to lie down on the carpet with him, which I did."

"Then his friends started to grab at me. I squirmed and tried to get away. But they held my arms and forced me to the floor. His one friend pulled my panties off while the other pushed my blouse up over my head."

"Once I was helpless on the floor they took turns raping me. They held me tightly by my arms and lifted my legs high up into the air and held them there. After they each had their fun Tommy turned me over and had anal sex with me. It hurt like hell as there was no lube. My crying meant nothing to him. They were all heartless bastards laughing as they continuously raped me that afternoon."

"When Tommy was finally done they picked me up and carried me to the front door and pushed me out into the hallway. My underpants were missing and my blouse was still pulled tightly over my head. When the door slammed shut I heard them laughing about what they did to me."

"I couldn't go home; and I was bleeding from my ass. My skirt was stained red and I didn't know how to stop the bleeding. I was crying and ashamed at what just happened to me. I was totally embarrassed and hurt. I was gang raped against my will; I could not stop crying as I walked to the stairway."

"Slowly I started to walk down the back stairs, one step at a time in great pain, hoping nobody would see me. This elderly Korean woman was walking down the staircase at that time and saw me. She asked me in Korean if I was okay. I started to cry uncontrollably and said no. She saw the blood all over my skirt and took me by my arm and slowly walked me down a flight of stairs to her young friend's apartment. She knocked on the door then used her key to open the lock and we entered the apartment together. She called to her friend and when we walked in this younger woman greeted us. Crying with tears running down my cheeks I told both of them what just happened in Tommy's apartment."

"They quickly undressed me and placed a large sterile cotton pad up my ass to stop the bleeding. They had me lie down on a bed in a side room when they paced it there. They saw that I was torn and bleeding very badly. They applied some Korean medicine they had to the bleeding and it slowed down and then stopped. The pain went away."

"Her friend made some Korean tea to calm me while the elderly woman covered me with a big warm blanket. I was shaking uncontrollably. Probably from shock as it was not cold in the apartment."

"I didn't know their names then, and they were very kind to me" she said. "They were just strangers who took pity on me."

Mei did know their names but was smart enough not to say who they were. She would then tell the group the rest of her experiences with them.

"The younger woman asked what apartment Tommy lived in and I told her. I was exhausted and I knelt down onto the floor and fell asleep, and I slept there through the afternoon and night. I think they put something in the tea because I felt very tired; and I really did need the rest after my ordeal that afternoon."

"When I woke up the next day the younger woman was gone. But the elderly one was sitting at the kitchen table drinking some Korean tea. She said I did not have to worry about those boys ever again. I did not understand why she said it but I thanked her for her kindness. I then realized I could not leave the apartment as I had no clothes, as mine were all stained from blood or torn off of my body by the boys. I told her I had nothing to wear as all my clothes were ruined by the boys yesterday."

"The elderly woman patted me on the head and took me into her friend's bedroom, opened a closet door, and told me to put on some of her clothes. They were a little big on me but she knew I had no other option. At least I was somewhat presentable. And they were all very fashionable outfits too!"

"For breakfast the elderly woman made some soup and banchan [side dishes] after I got dressed."

"As I was sitting there I asked why the boys would not bother me again."

"The old woman smiled at me, waited a moment before she spoke again, and then said that she was a retired madam."

"The night hours and stress were too much for her at her advanced age so her young friend took over her business. The younger woman was her best working girl and a trusted friend and lover. They made an arrangement with each other. The elderly lady gave her the business and in return the girl would take care of her in her old age. The younger girl rents an apartment for her a few floors up, she said, and she pays for her rent and living expenses too. That was their deal."

When Mei had previously told the two women what had happed the younger woman left the apartment after Mei fell asleep. She went to make a phone call at a pay phone down the street. Mei never knew what happened due to that phone call.

In twenty five minutes a black Mercedes had pulled up to the apartment house and three big Korean men got out and went upstairs. Their tee shirts were stretched tightly from their bulging chest muscles as they stood on the sidewalk for a moment. They quickly walked into the lobby and up the back stairway taking two steps at a time to Tommy's apartment and knocked on the door.

Without thinking Tommy opened the door slowly. The first man then kicked it wide open and the three men strode in and stood in the living room staring at the three high school boys.

"Who is Tommy" the first one asked with a slight Korean accent. Tommy said he was and then started to back away. He sensed something bad was about to happen to him.

Each of the men immediately took a boy by the hair and proceeded to bitch slap him three or four times until they dropped to their knees on the floor with broken jaws and blood gushing from their noses.

The first man then picked up his boy and took him into the bathroom. He told him he was very upset at what he did to a young Korean girl and he has to be punished for it. He then flipped open the toilet seat, grabbed the kid by the hair on the scruff of the neck and plunged his head, face down, into the toilet holding him there as he thrashed about. When the bubbles finally stopped and his body stopped moving, he lifted his head up and threw him down on the floor. Ever so slightly his chest was moving, as he was gasping for air. Then he was kicked in his crotch with a massive kick that sent him hurling into the corner of the bathroom, his face bouncing off of the pink porcelain bathtub so hard that his eyes actually swelled shut immediately.

The second man took his boy into the bedroom and just kicked and punched him until he was a bloody mess. His face was covered in blood and he had a collapsed lung from a punch to his rib cage. Barely breathing he was stretched out on the floor writhing in pain.

The third man, the one in charge who had a five inch scar on the right side of his neck, had forcefully karate kicked Tommy in his chest. Tommy flew backwards and collapsed on the floor facedown with his arms and legs extended out. Then the man placed his right foot on Tommy's back holding him there until the other two men were finished. Once the three men were all together they all lifted Tommy up and escorted him to the stairway. They threw him down the first flight of stairs, and repeated it for every flight going down until they were on the ground floor. After the last flight of stairs Tommy was motionless and curled up in a fetal position, writhing with pain, on the hard cold black and white checker board tiled floor of the landing. They picked him up again, this time by his pants belt and walked out of the building. They threw him into the open trunk of their car.

The men drove through the back streets until they arrived in Bayside Queens. They stopped in the rear of a Korean restaurant that the Madam had owned and parked the car very close to the rear kitchen entrance. They all got out of the car, looked around to make sure no one was watching, and then they quickly opened the trunk. Tommy was pulled out of the trunk by his hair, dragged on the gravel, and brought into the rear kitchen. The cooks were waiting, very large pots were boiling water and the ovens were turned on high. The long stainless steel table was empty of pots and pans with assorted knives hanging from above. Tommy was never seen or heard from again.

"So what happened next after you got dressed?" Dawn asked Mei.

"Well... I had nowhere to go. After what I did to my step father I couldn't go back home. I had to live somewhere so the elderly lady suggested that I move in with her and she would take care of me. So I did that, I had no other option. The apartment was really neat. It was painted in all light blue with a soft pastel green accent and furniture. I really found it relaxing. After a while I actually felt comfortable living there with them."

"And the police never found you?" Jose asked.

"Not at that time. Later they did. I lived with the elderly woman for a few months while I was recuperating. When I was feeling better she took me clothes shopping after dark at the large shopping malls in the suburbs, in Nassau County, and not in the neighborhood where I could be recognized. It looked like a grandmother was shopping for her granddaughter. After every purchase I kissed her thank you and she smiled at me each time. She had two large men, who were her driver and bodyguard; they would take us in a black Mercedes on these outings."

"I liked the shopping trips and was able to get a whole new closet full of clothes. Whatever I wanted she bought me. I loved to shop at the designer shops and at the boutiques. Even the big department stores had clothes and shoes I loved."

"Once she even had taken me to the golden mile in Long Island. There were a lot of expensive shops there and I could buy whatever I wanted. I didn't go crazy buying stuff because I realized it was her money, not mine."

"I had no time to myself as she was always with me. Yes she took care of me, very good care like I was her daughter. It's just that I missed my friends and doing something else besides watching television and shopping for clothes."

"I was now feeling much better. One day I was talking to the elderly woman about maybe going to California where there is another large Korean population, and living there. But I needed money to get there and I was only thirteen, almost fourteen by then."

"She suggested that I start working in one of the brothels she had owned. She would protect me and make sure I got my money, and not be cheated."

"So you worked in a whore house?" Dawn asked.

"Yes, but they had to train me. I was only with Tommy that once, and being raped by Young-soo was not exactly proper training on how to do it right. I agreed to it and that afternoon we went down stairs to the younger woman's apartment after lunch. She had just woken up and was having her morning tea when we walked in" Mei said.

"The elderly woman explained what she had suggested to me and then Semmi smiled."

Not realizing that she had mentioned a name inadvertently, she continued her story using the younger woman's name.

“Semmi smiled at me and took me by my hand as we walked into her bedroom. The room was painted red with red carpeting. It was very thick and I felt like I was sinking in with every step I took. Her bedroom furniture was all white with red trim around the edges.”

She didn’t bother to close the door behind us. There was no need to as the elderly woman came into the room with us.”

“She explained to me that we were going to have sex and as we did she would be teaching me what to do, and how to do it properly.”

“Semmi said that I was not selling my body, but my time. The quicker the man came the quicker I could get to the next guy. That was how I would make a lot of money both for her and for myself.”

“The elderly lady took out a bottle of perfume from a drawer and sprayed very expensive perfume on my neck and crotch. She said that if I sprayed my crotch the scent would travel up, and my whole body would smell nice.”

“Semmi opened the top drawer on her nightstand and took out a tube of lube and a large purple electric penis as I just stood there not knowing what she was going to do with it.”

“Pulling me close to her Semmi placed her right hand behind my head and gently pulled me towards her. She told me that was how I was to embrace a client. She then kissed me softly on the lips and told me to open my mouth when we kissed. She kissed me again and this time she put her tongue into my mouth and slowly moved it around.”

“I did the same to her, and I said nothing.”

Everyone in the group sat motionless listening to Mei tell her story. No one spoke.

“Semmi started to unbutton her pajama blouse and dropped it to the floor” Mei continued. “She was not wearing anything else. I noticed that her hair was trimmed very short down there. I never knew that you were supposed to trim it. I just stood there watching her. Silently without saying anything to me she started to undress me and then we both went over to the bed and sat down on it."

"Speaking softly Semmi explained to me that sex was a business, but it could be pleasurable too… if done correctly."

"She gently took me in her arms, embraced me, and started to kiss me again. Slowly she started to kiss my neck, then down my chest to my small breasts. Kissing and licking them she then placed her hand between my thighs and started to excite me. I had to remember everything she did to me. This was my schooling and I had to learn it correctly" Mei told them.

"As I was starting to move she stopped and pointed to the items she had taken out of her top drawer. She explained that using the lubricant I could have many men and not feel sore; even if they had sex with me in my ass."

"Semmi picked up the electric penis and placed a lot of lubricant on it, turned it on and slowly inserted it into my vagina while it was turning."

Doctor Willentz was mesmerized by this conversation and did not stop her. No one in his many years of practice had ever described to him how they were voluntarily seduced.

"My body" Mei was saying, "reacted to the insertion automatically and started to move up and down. I began to moan and my hips started to push downwards more forcefully. I started to lose control and I had an unbearable rush through my body that I had never experienced to that degree before."

"Semmi saw me moving and waited until I had a few orgasms. Then she put more lubricant on it and turned me over and slowly started to insert it in my ass."

"She explained that men will pay a lot extra for this. But they have to be well lubricated, and that you have to first insert a dildo yourself to loosen the anus so it would not hurt, she told me."

"I was very excited by Semmi; and then the old lady started to kiss me and she pulled me to the side of the bed and started to lick me down there also" Mei said as she continued her story. "I had sex with both of them that afternoon, and I really enjoyed it."

"After an hour or so of this Semmi felt that I was ready and told me to get dressed and I would come to work with her that night."

"I was really tired from having sex with the two of them but I couldn't refuse to go. I had a good time that afternoon and thought it would continue when I got to her place in Manhattan."

"Her driver and a bodyguard picked us up in a black Mercedes with tinted windows and drove us to 32nd street in Manhattan. I never saw the driver before and he was a very powerful looking man. Actually I thought he was scary looking because he had a large scar on his neck and huge muscles."

"When we finally got to Manhattan he stopped in front of a small run down looking building and parked in a no parking zone. I got out of the car with the bodyguard and Semmi and I followed him as we went through a plain steel entry door and up a flight of stairs. The hallway was not well lit and the paint was not peeling but looked faded. There was a smell in the hallway of body odor but I kept walking and said nothing. I walked behind him as we walked up three flights and into a door with the number seven on it. But there were only two doors on that floor."

Mei explained to everyone that "in Korea the number seven is a lucky number so we put it on doors even if it doesn't apply."

"I went in and there were three older girls sitting around, dressed in tight jeans and tube tops. Two of them were Korean and one was a small chubby white girl who Semmi had picked up at the 42nd street bus station a few months before. She introduced me to the girls and they were all very friendly. Although I was competition they quickly realized that I was someone very special to Semmi as she kissed me good luck."

"The two older Korean girls were in their late twenties and had been working for Semmi for a few years already. I spoke to them later that day and they told me how the rotation worked and how much to charge. I really had no idea how much money I could make there, but they clued me in. It was a lot of cash, and I had to split it with Semmi."

"Semmi pulled me aside and told me that Min-jun was her trusted assistant, sometime lover, and was parking the car. When he came back, she said, he would be my first. She informed me he was one of her many boyfriends and a trusted bodyguard and that he would be gentle with me. Also she said that he was large and if I could do him then I would not have any problems with other men."

Dawn piped in "Was he really large? How big was he?" She asked.

"That is not relevant" Dr. Willentz said. "We are here to learn about Mei's life, what brought her here, and how we, together, can help her."

"I worked there for two years until I was almost sixteen" she continued. "I moved in with Semmi and we became lovers. It was great as I went to a lot of fun parties with her if we were not working. But the parties became sort of work too. It depended on the men who were there and who was throwing the party. Sometimes I had to go into a bedroom with different men during the night. One night at a party I did almost twenty guys. I liked the older guys as they were slower and a lot gentler. The younger studs wore me out fast and they sometimes became very rough; but not to the point where I was in pain. They were quick tricks though. And the booze and food they had were always tops."

"Semmi had a lot of corporate executives who were clients and they would hire us to entertain their customers, especially the Midwestern guys from the farm belt states. Often the corporate guys would go to a major hotel and take over a larger suite with unlimited food and liquor. The suites were always on an upper floor with spectacular views of Manhattan at night. They had to impress their customers. Sometimes they had a live band in the suite and the parties would really get crazy. I had a ball doing a lot of those parties."

"Didn't the other hotel guests sometimes complain about the noise" asked Amanda.

"Yes, sometimes they did. But either one of Semmi's girls or I would give the night manager oral sex and he would leave us alone" Mei responded.

"We also went to the Hamptons during the summers with Min-jun on weekdays, because weekends were money days for us."

"Semmi would usually stay with one of her favorite clients when she went out there. He was an internationally known high fashion designer and Semmi would stay with him for a week or two while his wife was in Europe or somewhere, and I would chill with Min-jun in the guesthouse on his beach front property."

"The designer always had parties in the evening with a lot of top name people who were always featured on the entertainment television shows. Sometimes the designer would have an assistant drive out from

Manhattan with free dresses and outfits for Semmi and me. It was really cool. And we got to keep them also!"

"Usually once a season Semmi would have another girl brought out to the Hamptons and the designer would have a party with the three of us girls. That was an easy party because he was older and never had enough energy to do all of us. So he usually concentrated on the new girl and left me pretty much alone."

"When we weren't in the Hamptons on business Semmi had her own place on Fire Island that she owned and she usually rented it out for July. If it wasn't rented she used to hang out there a lot during the summers and bring a bunch of us along for a short vacation. Semmi had a few girls brought in and her parties were wild. By then I was already bisexual and I had a blast at the summer house on Fire Island" Mei told everyone.

"At the Fire Island beach house I used to walk around naked all the time and hang out on the front deck smoking weed. Once in a while a cute guy would walk by and stop to talk to me; and if I really liked him I'd invite him in for a private party with me, at no charge. It would be just the two of us. And I really had fun with the twinkies who were really young and inexperienced. They were great to screw around with; they never ran out of steam and could go for hours. There were also a lot of cute lesbians on the island and sometimes Semmi and I had a threesome together. It was a blast".

Mei continued on…"On a Monday morning a few years ago the New York City Police Department changed precinct captains around and the new precinct commander raided Semmi's place on 32nd street. Fortunately Semmi wasn't there that day. She was at one of her places in Bayside Queens."

"But I was there and they booked me for prostitution. That wasn't so bad until they asked for my name. They ran it through the system and found a warrant for my arrest for the murder of my stepfather" Mei told them.

Nobody said a word, not even Dawn. They just sat quietly and listened to her tell her life story.

"Immediately they segregated me from the adult population and sent me to a juvenile detention center in Brooklyn. It was a secure facility as I was wanted for murder and they didn't want me getting away."

"Semmi was not too upset about her place being raided", Mai continued. "She had a few others and was even thinking of moving from that place on 32nd street to a nicer location downtown, near the New York Stock Exchange. She had a lot of older brokers as customers in her other uptown New York brothel and figured she would get a younger and richer customer coming to see her girls if she opened one near the battery."

"But she was very upset that I was arrested for murder, although she knew all about it from years ago when we first met. I was her young lover and she took good care of me. She called her lawyer, Yossie Gootman from Brooklyn, and he represented me at my bail hearing" Mei told everyone.

"When I was brought into court Mr. Gootman was my lawyer and he was waiting for me. He told the judge that I was a thirteen year old juvenile at the time, was repeatedly raped by my stepfather, and was kind and good to my mother. He asked that my case be sent to family court although I was only days away from being eighteen."

"The assistant district attorney did not object and the judge was okay with the request. I was led out in handcuffs and was to be sent back to Brooklyn until my case was heard in family court. The judge refused to set bail as at that time I had no standing in the community, was working as a prostitute, had no assets that could be found, and no family there to vouch for me at the time of my bail hearing. My mother needed a translator so she was not able to speak at the bail hearing."

"When I was led out of the court building I had to go through the basement where there were plenty of holding cells with all kinds of weirdo's calling out to me. I was being brought to the juvenile detention center in Brooklyn and was sent with two court officers in an unmarked police car."

"One was an older guy in his late forties and he sat in the back seat with me. The younger officer was driving. The officer sitting next to me asked if I would like a cigarette and I said yes. By that time I smoked cigarettes and weed and did some light drugs too."

"The police car had already left the court house and we were driving to the detention center when he propositioned me."

"Well if I do something good for you, he said to me as he unzipped the front of the yellow jumpsuit that I was wearing and began fondled my small tits, what are you going to do for me?"

Mei continued her story "he unzipped his pants and whipped it out expecting me to satisfy him".

She stopped talking for a few seconds and just sat there quietly… with everyone waiting for her to continue.

"Yer, so I did it as we were on the Manhattan Bridge going back to Brooklyn. My hands were cuffed behind my back and it was hard for me to move around in the backseat. So he had lowered my face into his crotch, unzipped his fly and took it out, and I did it to him on the bridge. When we drove off the bridge and hit the streets his partner, a younger cop about twenty five or so who was driving, pulled into a big parking lot off of Flatbush Avenue, just past Atlantic Avenue. He flashed his badge to the parking attendant, and drove to the rear of the lot. The parking attendant never said a word and just let he drive in. He pulled in to a spot between two big suv's where nobody could see what was going on. We were surrounded by dozens of empty parked cars. The two officers got out of the car and changed places. The younger cop got in the back seat with me and asked if I would like a full pack of cigarettes as he pulled me closer to him. He didn't even wait for an answer when he went to kiss me and stuck his tongue into my mouth."

"Both of them were horny bastards. They knew I was initially arrested for prostitution so he offered me the full pack of cigarettes if he could screw me. I was almost eighteen by then and I had no real choice in the matter anyway, so I said yes. I was in a one piece prison jumpsuit and he didn't want to uncuff me. So he had me stand up and lean over the back of the front seat. He took out his pocket knife, grabbed the jumpsuit by my inner thighs and pulled it downwards, and then he cut a hole in the crotch of my uniform. He inserted his finger through the hole while I was bent over and into my vagina. He tried to masturbate me so I would get wet and make it easier for his dick to slide in. When he thought it was wet enough he lifted me up a little and placed me on his lap. Then he screwed me through that cutout he made."

"I had to jump up and down until he came. I was sweating as they kept the windows up so nobody heard us. It was hot as hell in there because the air conditioning was not strong enough to reach the back seat; and my hair was matted together from my sweat."

"When he was finished nailing me I was then driven to juvee jail and handed over to the receiving officer there. I was again finger printed and then processed in. A female officer said I had to shower and change into a clean jumpsuit. They brought me to a cinderblock holding room with a shower in it with no curtains. I had to shower with this old butch policewoman, with a very short man's haircut, watching me. I was washing myself off as best I could and tried to get that assholes sperm out of me by fingering myself. She smiled as I did this and she never took her eyes off of me, not even once."

"That bitch had taken my jumpsuit and inspected it before my shower and she noticed the large irregular hole in the crotch with wet sperm still on the inside of it. That female guard watched my every move but never said anything. I think she knew what had happened in the police car but did not want to turn the court officers in. And to top it off she took that pack of cigarettes away also."

"After the shower the butch guard had me step out of the water area and she put on a thick rubber glove and began a deep cavity search of my vagina and ass. She smiled as she inserted her finger into my vagina and started to twist her middle finger around, trying to arouse me. She pulled me closer to her as she did this and began to lick my lower stomach and then my clit. Quickly she started to suck on it like a vibrator and I got really aroused. We were the only ones in the shower section when she did that."

"Then with her other hand she grabbed my ass and turned me around. I had to bend over so she could do an anal cavity search. Then she inserted her fat pudgy finger into my ass; but I felt no pain when she did that as both holes were very stretched out by then. It was just like another day at the office for me" Mei said matter of factly. "When she was finished she laughed and thanked me. That bitch got off on doing that to me, I know it."

"But you do sleep with girls, don't you?" Amanda asked.

"Yes but I like soft girls, pillow princesses. Not hard core dykes. They are too rough for me" she answered her.

"I was there in the detention center for three months until my case was called. When the police came to bring me back to court it was two different officers and this time nothing happened. I think they knew I was going to court to see my lawyer so they didn't want to screw around with me."

"When I arrived at family court Mr. Gootman and I sat in a small office the court provided for us so we could speak privately. There was a large table with four or five chairs in the room. The windows had bars on it and if we had to leave the room we had to knock on the door and a court officer would unlock it before opening the door. I told Mr. Gootman in detail what had happened at home, how and why I killed my stepfather, and that I was also raped for years by him. He wrote everything I said down on a large yellow pad and then he put it in his brownish worn looking leather briefcase."

"He was not a fancy dresser as his suit was a little creased looking ; but Semmi told me he had years of criminal court experience and was probably one of the best in the city."

"Semmi had arranged for him to speak to my mother the week before I saw him and she confirmed what I had just told him. My mother had saved the note that I written to her before I left. She also at that time had the police read it and they wrote what I said in my letter to her into their report. My mother told Mr. Gootman through a translator that she was willing to testify in court about the abuse she suffered from her husband, and what she knew of my being raped by him."

"My Mom said she had been aware of it but was afraid to say anything as he had brutally beaten her so many times, and sent her to the hospital with severe injuries. She was afraid for her life if she said anything to the police, or to him, plus she spoke very little English."

"When I walked into court that day I told my story to the judge and my mother, with the help of a court certified translator, also testified. But I had still murdered my stepfather. I really don't understand the rest of what happened there was so much legal bullshit being said, but I was sentenced to jail to one to two years, then probation".

"Did they send you to a prison?" Jose asked. He had spent some time in a prison in New Jersey, East State prison to be exact.

"No, they kept me in Juvee for a year until I was released for good behavior and time served in holding. Semmi came to visit me often and my mother too" Mei told the group.

"Semmi made sure I had money in my jail account for extras if I wanted something. It wasn't too bad being there. Some of the new black girls that were brought in were street hos and really rough but I got along with them. I was on the smaller side so I kept my distance."

"Once they put this big black hoe, Tamika, in my cell with me for a few months. She initially had an attitude and I thought I was going to have trouble with her, but she turned out to be a really sweet girl. She just looked tough as shit with all her tattoos and piercings, but when I started to talk to her, she was real."

"Tamika also was abused as a young girl. Her mother's boyfriends used to have sex with her after they paid her mother to be with Tamicka. No shit" Mei said to the group, "her own mother used to pimp her out. Also while they were in the mother's apartment they did drugs with her and her mom. We actually had a lot in common when we sat down and started to talk to each other."

"She was fifteen but really tall and skinny and looked like she was in her mid-twenties. After a few days we became good friends. On her third night there after lights out I sneaked into her bunk and we had sex, kissing and getting each other off. Being that she was a big girl I used her as my bodyguard while I was in the jail. She kept the nasty butch lesbians away from me."

"This guard was walking by our cell one evening and he stopped by our cell door. He looked at us kissing and he escorted us out of our cell and walked us to the officer in charge's private office. He explained to the lieutenant on duty what we were doing."

"The lieutenant then made us an offer. Either have sex with him and the guard right there or he'll put us in solitary until our case comes to trial. So we knelt down and we blew both of them. Then we had to get out of our jumpsuits and bend over onto his desk. They each screwed us and when they were finished, they had us blow them again."

"Finally we were walked back to our cell. But almost every other day or so both of us were walked in to the office to be with a different guard. Even some of the butch female guards came to watch; and one or two of them even at times started to lick us and had us perform oral on them too! It was a hell hole in that juvee place. Anything went; there was nothing off limits because we were kids."

"Tamika's last pimp was her mother's boyfriend and would beat her if she didn't turn enough tricks for him. He had her working Hunts Point and also 8th

Avenue in Manhattan. They were really tough hoe meat markets where she had a lot of competition turning tricks. That was where Tamicka was arrested; she solicited an undercover cop. Her pimp never bailed her out. Her mother said she broke up with him and threw his ass out the door and he disappeared."

"I really liked talking to her and told her where I worked. It was relatively safe and she wouldn't get beat on or shit like that. I still mistakenly thought I had a year or so to go before I got out. I knew she would be out pretty soon, once her bail was posted."

"I called Semmi and told her I had to see her tomorrow. She came to juvee to see me and I spoke to her and told her about Tamika."

"That afternoon Semmi bailed her out and Tamika started immediately to work for Semmi in one of her houses in Bensonhurst Brooklyn. It was a predominantly Italian trade there and she could make a lot of money at that location. Those wannabe mafia types loved young black girls with big boobs."

"She was put in a newer place where there weren't so many Koreans. She did well there for Semmi and when her case came to court she was sentenced to time served. Semmi made sure that Gootman was her lawyer also. Gootman made sure that Tamika's mother was in court that day. She vouched for Tamika thinking her new pimp would get her back to working the streets. But Tamika never went back home. As soon as she walked out of court with her mother Min-jun and two of his men were waiting for her. He approached Tamika and her mother and stood in front of them so they could not pass. Min-jun gently took Tamika by her arm and walked her to the car. He opened the car door for her to get in. She turned around and said goodbye to her mother, sat down in the car and Min-jun drove her away in Semmi's black Mercedes."

“No shit” Jose said. “You recruited for her too?”

“I don’t think of it that way. I was just trying to help two people I liked” Mei said.

“So how did you end up in here?” Dawn asked.

Barbara just sat there listening. Not saying anything. She was still too embarrassed to tell her life story to these strangers. It would take a little more time until she felt more comfortable with them.

“Don’t pressure her” Doctor Willentz said. “She is doing just fine. All of you have to acknowledge what the problem is before you can correct it. Please go on Mei.”

She continued “when I was released a little while later I walked out of the detention center and Semmi and Min-jun were waiting for me. She had traded in the Mercedes and bought a new big ass Cadillac SUV in white with chrome wheels and very dark tinted windows. I got in the rear seat with her and we started to kiss on the way back to her place. Semmi spoke to me in Korean and said she had missed me a lot and was glad we were together again.”

“Semmi told me she had moved from the apartment in Queens to a bigger one in Manhattan; into a very nice building with a doorman and underground parking with an elevator in the garage. This was helpful when select clients wanted to visit her and bypass the doorman and security cameras. The elderly madam was still living in her old apartment house in Queens. She liked the neighborhood with the many Korean shops located there and didn’t want to leave it. Semmi still paid her rent and supported her” Mei told the group.

“When I walked into Semmi’s new apartment I was greeted by a short, middle aged, over weight Jewish woman with blond hair named Brianna Jacobs. That was how Semmi introduced me to her.”

"Brianna was a receptionist for Semmi's new escort company and she handled the phones in a small bedroom office and also made the arrangements for the girls. She also tracked their bookings. Not a particularly good looking woman but adequate at her job" Mei said in an even tone of voice. "Her neck skin would hang from under her chin and she always wore too much makeup, and…she had pudgy short fingers too."

"Semmi was opening a lot of new locations and was attracting more moneyed men and even a few women, too. She had me start back in one of her better houses to get adjusted to that life style again. Then after two weeks she had me go to clubs in Manhattan to pick up and find high end clients. I was kind of a finder for her."

"I liked that" Mei said.

"I was dressed in highly fashionable clothes and they were extremely tight fitting so I never wore any undergarments. I have very small tits and they just pointed out a little from the dress. Dancing and drinking into the night was a lot of fun. It was there I met this great looking white guy. His name was Eddie and he was in advertising with some very large Madison Avenue company with offices nationwide."

"He was the manager for their public relations political department. His company was very active with political parties and candidates and had a lot of clients all around the country, even in California. We had met at a club in the meat market area in Manhattan when he walked over and stood next to me. He bought me a drink at the bar without even asking me what I was drinking."

"I was wearing a tight fitting bright red silk dress that was low cut and there were no panty lines popping out from any underwear. It couldn't as I wasn't wearing any then either. And my nipples were staring at him as I wasn't wearing a bra. That helped a lot, especially when I started to dance and sweat, and my dress clinged to my tiny girls."

"The music was very loud and the dance floor was packed. So I sat down at a small table to rest for a second."

"After noticing me and buying me that drink he kept looking me over for a while until he came up to me as I sat there and he asked me to dance. But I was looking for more than a dance, he was so hot looking. I smiled at him, stood up and took him by his hand and we walked to the back of the club. We went right into the ladies room together. He seemed a little uneasy following me when we walked in there, but I kept focused and continued walking in, dragging him behind me. We ignored the other women in the bathroom. I took him to the back area and into a larger handicap stall, locked the solid wooden door to the stall behind us, and then I turned around and started to kiss him. He placed his hand on my lower stomach and slid it down between my legs. I hiked up my dress and bent over. He knew what to do next. After that I knew I had hooked him in and after he finished I turned around, put my hand behind his head and pulled his lips to mine. Then we walked out of the stall and went back out to the dance floor. We were ignoring the girls in the rest room that were staring at us as we passed by them going to the door. I never said anything to Eddie, just actions."

"We spent the rest of the evening dancing together and when it was time to leave he asked me for my phone number. I gave him Brianna's service number. I told him it was my office number and to ask for Mei and leave a message. He gave me his business card and walked me out to the sidewalk. We stood there making small talk while I waited for my ride to arrive."

"A big white Cadillac SUV with oversized eighteen inch fully chromed wheels pulled up in front of us. Min-jun got out and opened the rear door for me to get in. He was wearing his tight fitting chauffeur's uniform that was conforming to his muscles. I turned and kissed Eddie good night on the lips while slipping my tongue into his mouth, and then I slid into the car. As Min-jun drove away I turned around and saw him standing there in amazement, looking at me drive away as we went uptown to Semmi's place."

Shaniqua turned to Mei and asked if she ever saw him again. As a Christian lady she could not believe what her ears were hearing. Although her life was very interesting also, she waited until it was her turn to talk.

"Yes" Mei said. "I saw him a lot on a steady basis after that night, and a few weeks later I told Eddie what I did for money. He just listened but was not surprised. He was rather pleased in that I never charged him for my time."

"I was living with Semmi and I was allowed to bring him into the apartment with me if she wasn't working there that evening. Sometimes he spent the night there with Semmi and I, all three of us in the same bed having sex. The shades were always pulled up at night. It was a nice apartment with floor to ceiling windows and great views of Manhattan. While we would be having sex on her bed the night lights of the other Manhattan buildings would shine in our window like little stars beaming at us. I really liked living there."

"Finally one night I told Eddie that he had to repay me for my favors and it would not cost him a penny. I knew he would do what I asked. Men can't say no after a great blow job."

"I told him the escort service I worked for was looking for some moneyed people and as he knew a lot of them I would like him to refer my service to his contacts. He agreed as long as I spent time with him and didn't leave him. I believe that he really liked me. I know I liked him a lot."

"In the weeks that followed Brianna started to get calls from politicians all over the country for personal consultants. As a consultant we were a tax write off. They flew us out to the many states where Eddie had contacts. But a lot of the out calls went to Washington D.C.; and the girls often just flew down that night to service the clients. Some of them took the train as it was less hassle than with the TSA inspecting their bags at the airports. It was not unusual for them to bring along toys and lube and their bags were never inspected on the trains."

"It didn't matter if they took the train to Union Station or the plane to Dulles. There was always a limo to drive them to their destination hotel."

"The politicians always took the girls to fancy hotels and had room service bring in dinner and drinks. The men were almost always married and did not want to be seen out with a young woman that was not their wife. They tried to avoid a scandal, but they couldn't stay away from the pretty girls."

"The biggest tipper was this conservative Republican Congressman from Texas. All the girls asked to date him for the night as he always left a few hundred on the dresser for them when he left."

"That was how I got really hooked on drugs. One day we got a call from a southern congressman and all the girls that didn't mind travelling were either out already or away on a paid escort trip to Europe. Semmi didn't want to send just any girl from her company so she asked me to fly down and service him."

"He sent a car service to pick me up from the airport and bring me to a fancy hotel downtown near the White House. His gay assistant Bernard met me at the door and brought me up to his room."

"How did you know he was gay?" asked Dawn.

Mei answered her "when he had better hair than me, wore his suit tightly fitted, and basically ignored me because I was going to sleep with his benefactor, sometimes you can tell, sometimes you can't. But that four eyed son of a bitch that never smiled at me was gay and probably jealous, too."

"Anyway Bernard told me that the senator liked to do certain things and there would be an extra thousand for me when he left. He and I walked to the hotel room door and knocked. This older gentleman with a full head of white hair that was brushed back opened the door, smiled at me, and asked me to come in. Bernard was left standing outside in the hallway when the door closed in his face."

"The congressman opened the thick white bathrobe that he was wearing when he greeted me at the door and dropped it to the floor. He had nothing on beneath it. He just stood there naked and smiled at me as if he did this every day."

"He turned around and motioned for me to walk behind him. I followed the congressman and we both walked into the dining alcove; and then he introduced himself by his first name. He asked me to undress and join him for dinner. So I took my clothes off in front of him and stood there for a moment while he inspected me."

"Didn't you feel embarrassed?" Amanda asked Mei.

'No, I really didn't. I had been with so many men by then that I really did not feel embarrassed in any way".

"Then he stepped towards me and embraced me. We started to kiss and I could feel him getting excited.

His cologne was very masculine and as he slid his tongue into my mouth his left hand started to rub between my legs. Just as I was starting to have tingling sensations shooting through my whole body… he stopped and pulled away from me."

"Dinner had been sent up for us" Mei continued, "and we both sat down at the table by the window overlooking the capital, completely naked and started to eat. We engaged in some small talk but it was about nothing, really. Small talk you know, how I liked my steak, how was my flight down; it was all about nothing that mattered. He would look up at me while he was eating every once in a while and smile. He had a full head of grey hair and gleaming white teeth. He really wasn't bad looking either for an older guy. That always helps the situation."

"As we were eating I thought that I recognized him. I remember thinking I saw his picture in the New York Post as a Family First Republican who was for family values, against abortions and same sex marriage. I guess adultery was okay. And let me tell you, he had a large package and was really kinky too."

"I really had nothing in common with him except we both wanted the same thing, sort of. He wanted sex and was willing to pay for it; I wanted his money and was willing to give him sex for it."

"After dinner we went to the bathroom where we took a shower together and soaped each other up. I lathered his body and washed his front and back really good. If I was going to lick it I wanted it very clean, especially his ass. He then washed me with his hands, not a wash cloth. He seemed to enjoy lathering my inner thighs up with a lot of soap as he rubbed his hands there and smiled. When we were finished we stepped out of the shower to dry off. He took the largest towel and hand dried me off everywhere he could think of, kissing all my body parts after he dried it. Then we went to the king sized bed in the adjoining room where he asked for oral sex, which I did while he sat on the edge of the bed. He lay back on the bed and rolled over onto his stomach. The congressman then asked me to insert something up his ass that he had laying on the night table after I put lube on it. He was a real nut job."

"After I did that he got up, thanked me, and he then poured wine for both of us. He gave me a full glass of red wine to drink. I was stupid and drank the whole glass. I think he must have put a date rape powder into my glass. I had no idea he was drugging me and it made me feel very tired. I thought it was the wine, but it wasn't."

"Then he took my hand and led me over to the bed and both of us laid down on it. He started to kiss me and fondle my breasts. He liked that they were not too large. I sort of remember he turned me over and said he was going to insert something into me. He put lube on his finger and he slowly inserted it into my ass. I don't remember too much of what happened after that, I must have blacked out. Why he drugged me I haven't the faintest clue as I was willing to do anything he wanted anyway."

"I awoke the next day about noon feeling very groggy, and my ass hurt like a bitch. He must have screwed me there a few times that night. I looked over at the dresser and he did leave me a thousand dollars in cash as a tip. I also saw a few crack rocks that he dropped on the floor; he must have dropped them during our romp that night. I knew what those rocks were, and I picked them up and I kept them."

"I barely was able to walk over to the bathroom and I took a short shower, trying to get the cobwebs out of my head. When I finished drying off and dressing I called down stairs for a taxi to take me to the airport.

But when I opened my door to leave Bernard was standing there waiting for me. He said he would drive me to the airport. The congressman had arranged for him to drive me. So I flew back to New York and I told Semmi what had happened to me. She never sent me to D.C. again after that trip."

"Over the next few weeks I took the crack rocks when I was with Eddie because they gave me an intense high that I never could achieve any other way. But I started to need more of them. I couldn't control myself and I felt very depressed when I wasn't high."

"Finally I showed the crack rocks to Eddie as I was running out of them and asked if he knew what they were. I played dumb but I knew he would know… and he had contacts everywhere that could help me score some more."

"Eddie said it was crack cocaine, which I already knew, and he said he knows where to get some for me. I really believe he was in love with me and would do anything I asked of him. I used him and he used me, but there was some emotion developing in me towards him that I had never felt with another man before."

"The last time I took some rocks I crashed really hard after we had sex and I was very depressed and suicidal. I was at Eddie' place on the Upper West Side of Manhattan that afternoon and he caught me just as I was going to jump from his apartment window. I was naked and crying as I opened the bedroom window."

"I had started to think of my mother and the life I had before I ran away, and I felt depressed and just had had enough of life."

"Eddie had no furniture in his bedroom except for a large king size bed. There was red carpeting on the floor with wall to ceiling mirrors on every wall in his bedroom, and on the ceiling too. I looked up at myself in the ceiling mirror while lying on his bed after getting screwed that afternoon; and at that moment I felt very depressed about what I did for money. I walked over to his window and opened it up all the way."

"I looked down to the sidewalk nineteen floors below and I as started to place one leg out the window Eddie walked out of the bathroom and into the bedroom. He saw what I was going to do and he ran right over to me and grabbed me just as I was about to leap out of the window. He pulled me to the floor and he laid his body on top of mine, pinning me to the floor and couldn't move. Eddie raised his voice and yelled at me never to do a crazy thing like that again. Then he said something to me that no one ever said. It really touched me because I knew he meant it."

"He told me he loved me and he held me tightly while we both lay on the floor with tears rolling down our faces. I was trembling and shaking and didn't want to let go of him. I can't really remember too much else of that moment, except I felt wanted, really wanted, by him."

"He said that I needed help and he would see that I got it. That's how I ended up here. He called Semmi and told her what had happened. She sent a private ambulance to Eddie's place for me. The ambulance took me to the hospital where they pumped my stomach and placed me in a mental ward. They gave me some drug to kill the high and strapped me to a bed. When Doctor Willentz came to see me he offered me this program. It sounded good and here I am" as Mei ended her story.

"Mei" Doctor Willentz asked, "How do you feel about Eddie?"

"I really like him, maybe even love him. He treated me with respect and no one else ever did. All the men I ever slept with really wanted just my body; but I felt Eddie really talked to me. He asked my opinion about things and no one ever did that before. I do miss him being in here. Or maybe I just miss the sex?"

"Do you think that what you miss is the human closeness, the emotional bond that you have for him, besides the sex?" asked Doctor Willentz.

Mei sat silently for a moment, thinking about what he said.

"Yes, it could be I miss him, and the sex. I enjoy being with him, but I like being with Semmi also. Maybe I have feelings for two people? I know one thing; I am not going to do crack again. When I was in the hospital I went through withdrawal and I can't go through that another time. That was the worst I ever felt" Mei told everyone.

"I realize I have too much in my life to lose" Mei answered.

"What do you mean by that?" ask Doctor Willentz.

"I guess if I am going to be really honest with you" she continued but Doctor Willentz interrupted her. "Mei, be honest with yourself, not us. That is really the most important part of your being here" he said to her.

"Then I guess I am in love with Eddie. I never had feelings for a man like I have for him. They were all just johns to me. They were meaningless men, one after the other. I had no feelings for any of them. But I know Eddie cares for me and understands my lifestyle. Not too many men would, I think" she said.

"But I have to work; I owe Semmi for giving me a life again, and I do love her also. I can't stop working for her just like that. Maybe I can cut back a little… but I don't know. Maybe…?" Mei told the group.

"I am not here to judge you Mei" Doctor Willentz told her. "You have to deal with your decisions in life. I am only here to try to guide you, not make them for you".

“Thank you Doc, I’ll see what I’ll do. I’m not sure of anything right now” Mei answered him.

Everyone was silent and just sat there thinking about their own issues and how they would deal with them when it was their turn to speak.

Doctor Willentz thanked her for being honest with herself and asked Dawn if she would like to continue.

Chapter Three – Dawn

Dawn was a young thirty something. She was a petite and average looking woman with mousy brown hair that was thinish and stringy; her hair laid flat with no waves or curls. It was kind of longish and went straight down past her ears. Her hospital gown hung on her skeletal body very loosely because she was severely malnourished and extremely thin.

Her face is plain, she wore no makeup and she had no outstanding features. She looked similar to the pictures one would see of depression era Americans who lost their Midwestern farms and were packing up to go to California.

“Dawn, if you would, please tell us something about yourself” Doctor Willentz asked in an even tone of voice.

“Okay,” she answered and then paused, took a deep breath and continued.

“I guess it all began when I was a teenager in middle school. Maybe it was in the seventh or eighth grade, I don’t remember exactly. I was an average student, my grades were decent, and I had a few good friends. There was one girl that I was very close to, Annette Marie. We lived two doors apart on our street. Her parents had a big Victorian home in Maplewood and my parents rented the second floor of a two family home on the same block” Dawn started her story with.

"I was always thin but in seventh grade Annette Marie started to grow her chest and fill out. My mother felt sorry for me so she bought me a training bra so I would not feel self-conscious, but it didn't work. I usually stuffed it with tissues that would fill it out more."

"Everything was okay until I had to go to gym class. I felt embarrassed and uncomfortable changing in front of the other girls. I really had no chest and the other girls were really filling out their bras. I was the only one in my class wearing a training bra and I felt embarrassed. So I volunteered to help in the attendance office during my gym class. When the attendance sheets came into the office I always changed my gym attendance to be present so it wouldn't get flagged."

Mei spoke up then. "I had the same problem but I never wore a training bra. Even today I often don't wear a bra. I feel closed in with it. Besides," she continued, "there's not much to hold up."

"I always wore a bra since I could remember" Shaniqua chimed in. "My sisters and I always had to wear one. We are packing big girls" she said.

"Me too" said Amanda. "Christ, I had to wear one! These things would go all the way to my waist if I let them" Amanda exaggerated. Although they were large, they pointed straight out and not down.

"I never wore one growing up" said Jose. Only when I hit my thirties and came out of the closet did I start to wear a bra. Then I started to wear one almost daily" he said, "especially when I was working."

Everyone looked at him but didn't say anything. They were trying to understand what he meant. Later he would explain everything to them in full detail.

Barbara never said a word. She just sat silently, stared at Jose, and listened.

"Dawn," Doctor Willentz said, "please continue."

"Okay," she answered, just above a whisper.

"High school wasn't too bad. A few of the older boys would tease me in the hall way. They called me mousey and would snap the bra strap on my back. To be honest, it stung and it kind of hurt my feelings; but I was kind of glad they even noticed me."

Amanda interrupted her, "did any boys ever ask you on a date in high school?" She asked.

"Just one boy asked me out in my junior year, his name was Marcus Abrams. He wasn't a very tall kid and he had short brown hair. I think it was some type of crew cut if I remember. We were in the same social studies class and he sat next to me. He always was looking at me and finally one day he got up enough courage and asked me out on a date."

"The next Saturday night he drove over to my house and picked me up in his car. We to see a movie in town and he put his arm around me in the theater."

"After it was over we drove to a diner on the highway and we each had a cheese burger with fries. I remember he had his with a large vanilla shake and he gave me the cherry that was on top. I ordered a grilled cheese sandwich with well-done fries and a large cola with extra ice. He was my only date while I was in high school" Dawn answered. "And I remember everything we did, down to the very last detail."

"Marcus wasn't too bad looking. The nerdy type with thick glasses and he always wore a pen in his shirt pocket. He worked part time in a local general store doing stock work after school. With the money he saved from that job he bought a ten year old used Ford convertible that he drove around in. It was blue, very dark blue, with white leather seats. I think it was leather, maybe it was vinyl. I really couldn't tell the difference. There was a large dent in the rear door and that was why he said he got a good deal on it. I really don't know much about cars but the upholstery wasn't torn or ripped or stained. I didn't get skeeved out or anything sitting in it" she continued.

"The first date went well. It was a Friday night and he kissed me goodnight. No tongue in my mouth or anything, and right there as I was putting my key in the lock to go inside, he asked me to go out with him the next night. I said yes. I had no one else knocking my door down, so I agreed to go out with him again. Why not, I thought?"

"He picked me up early the next night and we drove to Wedgewood where there was a drive-in movie on route 46. It was a very large drive in movie that seemed to have a parking lot that was a mile wide. I don't remember what was playing but we parked in the back and Marcus put the speaker in the front window."

"Then he got out, said he was going to the concession stand for hot dogs, soda and popcorn and asked me if there was anything I wanted besides that. I said no, that what he was going to get was okay with me. When he came back to the car carrying two drinks and a cardboard tray with food piled high on it, he asked me to get in the back seat where it was more comfortable to watch. So we both went in the back, and it was totally dark out already and then the movie started."

"We squished in together, sitting close to each other, and both of us ate the hotdogs; and then we sat back to watch the movie."

"Marcus put his arm out and pulled me over to him, we were now even closer to each other. We made out a little, he slipped his tongue in my mouth and I was kind of shocked. I never had that happen to me before. I saw kissing in the movies when I went with my girlfriends but I never personally experienced romantic kissing with anyone. After a few minutes of making out

Marcus then he put his hand where I was never touched before…and I liked it. At first I was uncomfortable with it but Annette had gone all the way with this boy she knew a few weeks before; and she told me what he did to her. So I had some idea of what to expect."

"I feel uncomfortable describing it like Mei did. I would rather not get into the real details about my first time, if that is okay with everyone?" Dawn asked.

Doctor Willentz confirmed to her that it was alright not to get too graphic if it made her feel uncomfortable. It was up to her, he said.

"Well, did you like it?" Shaniqua asked.

"I don't know. It was kind of awkward doing it in the back seat. I was scrunched up and had to lift my legs up a bit. It hurt a little as I wasn't too excited. My nerves were all tensed up and I was kind of rigid, I think. I just remember I had to lie down on the back seat and he really did the rest. I do remember he lifted my skirt up and pulled my panties down and took them off of me. But that's about all I do remember of it, to be honest with you. I closed my eyes, felt him enter me, and it was over really quick and fast" she answered.

"When he was finished he gave me the napkins from the concession stand that came with the hot dogs so I could clean myself up a little. When I was finished, after a few minutes wiping myself clean, we sat together and watched the movie till it finished."

"Afterwards he took me home and kissed me goodnight in the car. While we were kissing he put his hand on my chest and he tried to feel my boobs. But before I left on the date that afternoon, when I was getting ready to go out, I anticipated that he would do that. My chest was very soft due to the tissues I had stuffed in them before I left the house. All he really felt in the car when he squeezed my boobs were tissues and cotton balls" Dawn told them.

"Did he ask you out again, or did he drop you after that night?" asked Amanda.

"No, I never saw him again. But it's not like what you think" Dawn responded.

"That night when he dropped me off I went upstairs and showered. I tried to get his stuff off of me, but I didn't realize that it was also in me! Then I went to my room and I laid down on my bed. I started to day dream about getting married to Marcus. I know it was foolish and little girlish, but he was the first boy to ever ask me out. And I had sex with him too, because I thought he liked me. Plus I also wanted the experience so I could compare notes with Annette Marie the next day after church. He did ask me out for another date when he dropped me off" she emphasized. "And we made out a little before he drove home."

"That night I started to draw hearts with arrows through them on my school notebook and I put both of our initials in the hearts. I couldn't wait to tell Annette when I saw her the next day that I went all the way with him."

"I over slept on that Sunday morning and I missed going to church with my family. I was bursting at the seams to tell my best friend about my first sexual experience, but it would have to wait till Monday morning when we went to school."

"After church my father always took the family out for a drive and we always had lunch at a diner on the highway."

"So when Annette and I left for school the following morning I told her all about my date with Marcus as we walked to the high school. I was on cloud nine and giddy as can be. I was in love, I thought."

"We went into school still talking about my car date with Marcus as we went into our homeroom. The speaker on the wall in the front of the classroom rang out with three tones and there was an announcement from the principal that every class had to go to the auditorium after the second period."

"So we went to the assembly together after second period. When Annette and I sat down on the old fold down oak seats the principal got up to speak. There were a few guidance teachers on the stage with him and a policeman. A lot of kids were whispering to each other. I couldn't make out what they were saying but I soon found out."

"The principal walked to the microphone and started to speak. Everyone stopped talking and sat still, waiting to hear what the principal was going to say. He told us that one of our fellow students was killed last night while driving home. A stolen car driven by two young boys from East Orange was being chased by the police. They went through a red light and broadsided the car driven by Marcus Abrams" he then paused and stopped talking for a second while we were in shock listening to him, "and he was killed."

"He wasn't wearing a seat belt and Marcus died from internal injuries when he was thrown from the car and it rolled over on him."

"I sat there in disbelief. This couldn't happen. In my mind I was going to marry him. I just had sex with him Saturday night. He couldn't be dead. No, no. It just can't be, I kept saying to myself."

"I must have zoned out as I don't remember walking out of the auditorium with Annette, or even the rest of the school day. When I got home from school that afternoon I ended up in my room and immediately fell asleep. That's all I can remember about that day."

"I think Marcus was Jewish because his funeral was the following day at a Jewish funeral chapel in the next town over. It didn't matter to me what he was when we were together. He was a boy and I was a girl. That was all that really counted then to me."

"My father was not religious at all. He went to church on Sundays with my mother because she made him go. If there was a Giants football game and he had tickets, he used that as an excuse not to attend church. Dad always bought season tickets high up because that was what he could afford, and he used to say the Giants got him out of going to church, so they were blessed."

"But mom was a real church goer. She was Italian and my father was something else. He never told me and I never asked. But my mother went to church every day in the morning, rain, snow or ice nothing kept her away from her church."

"Ya know that was her life and I had to lead my own life. I thought I was a good daughter. My older two sisters always did what mom wanted them to do. I did too, most of the time. But I never really liked going to church. For some reason it didn't click with me. Too much hocus pocus and stuff. Besides my real concern was how much bigger my boobs would get! God had other things to be concerned about, was my way of thinking, and I had my boobs to worry about. I was desperately waiting for my breasts to start growing."

Everyone sitting in the semi-circle with Dawn all laughed when she said that. The laughter made her feel a little more relaxed and comfortable with the group.

Dawn continued speaking. "For the next month or so everything kind of went back to normal. I went to high school in the morning with my friend Annette Marie and worked in the office instead of going to gym."

"Then one morning I woke up and ran to the bathroom and threw up. My mother thought I had a stomach virus so she made me some toast and hot tea to try and calm my stomach down. I didn't have a fever so she told me I had to go to school."

"That night when I sat down for dinner I started to dry heave at the table and my mother got up from her chair and ran over to me and felt my head. I was cool. I said I was feeling better and finished my dinner."

"This happened to me a few more times that week and I started to get headaches more frequently, especially in the afternoons, but I ignored them. When I was getting dressed in the morning one day I noticed that my boobs were getting bigger and I started to have a small belly bump."

"I told Annette on our way to school and she said I was pregnant. I didn't believe her. I only had sex once with Marcus, I told her, how could that happen? But it did" Dawn told the group.

"I was in a panic. I didn't know what to do. I thought my mother would kill me when she found out. She was a real holy roller and I didn't know what my father would say either. But I figured I had to tell them and whatever they did to me was Gods will. At that moment I got really religious."

"At dinner that night I waited till everyone was seated and started to eat. I figured with a full mouth they wouldn't be able to yell at me too much. So I finally got up enough courage to tell them I was pregnant. Each of my parents sat at the far ends of the table in silence. They stopped eating and looked at each other in disbelief. I figured they were too far away to reach over and slap me, and my older sisters sat between them and me, so when they had finished saying grace and started to eat I thought it was a good time to let them know their mousey daughter was pretty enough to get knocked up."

"My mom was shocked and started to yell at me how could I do this to her. My dad just sat there and said nothing. My two older sisters also started to yell at me that they would never get married now that everyone in town would know I was a tramp. Who would want to marry into a family like ours now, they said".

"The hysterics went on for almost thirty minutes until my father finally quieted everyone down and said he would take care of it. We were not to tell anyone, and he emphasized ***anyone***. He had a friend at work whose daughter had been in the same situation, he told us. He sent her away to have the baby and put it up for adoption."

"My sisters stood up, said I had better not tell anyone, and they left the room pissed as hell at me. My mom asked if my dad knew where that girl was sent and he said he would find out tomorrow at work."

The group was silent as they listened to Dawn tell her story. They did not want to interrupt her as they saw she was welling up with tears and started to speak ever so lower that they had to strain to hear her.

"My dad came home the next day and said he found out where his friend's daughter was sent when she got pregnant. Dad had already made arrangements over the telephone for me before he even came home."

"Mom now went to church in the morning *and* in the afternoon. I think if she could she would have moved in to the church" Dawn told them.

"I was to tell everyone that I was being sent to a private boarding school in Florida for my education. So the next day my dad telegraphed money from Western Union to the school in Florida and he bought me a plane ticket on Red-Jet Airlines to fly to Fort Lauderdale."

"My mom packed a suitcase for me and put in it what she thought I would need to wear in Florida. The next day my dad drove me to Newark Airport early in the morning; and he waited with me until I boarded the plane. The stewardesses were very nice and they made sure I was seated and comfortable. They watched over me the whole flight as I was still a minor."

"While my dad and I were sitting and waiting in the airport terminal he asked me if I could keep a secret. I said yes, and I saw tears welling up in his eyes as he turned to me. Then he told me that my mom and he had been in a similar situation. They both were too young to get married and raise a family, so mom moved to Minnesota with an elderly aunt until the baby was born; and then she gave it away for adoption. She never heard from the baby again and her aunt never mentioned it to anyone in the family. It was a little boy. He was the only son I ever had."

"Dad said he remembers that mom got very religious after that. Going to church was her way of asking for forgiveness from Jesus for giving away her baby son. It helped her mind settle any misgivings and self-guilt she might have had."

"I was really shocked when my father told me, to say the least. In all honesty I don't know if he made that up to calm my nerves or it was a true story. I couldn't believe that is what he said to me. And I would never dare to ask my mother. Yes… it kind of helped me cope with my situation a little, but not much. I was very nervous and afraid. But I got on the plane and went to Florida to have my baby…and give it away."

"The school had someone meet me at the airport and then take me to the boarding school. The place was not bad looking when I first saw it. It looked very Floridaish with white columns and a sun porch and peach trim. The head master had me escorted to my room after I met with her in the main office downstairs on the first floor. She gave me a guide book of rules of the school that I was to read."

“My room was clean, painted a very light blue, and it had an off white shade that I could pull down to block the sun. There was a fan over my bed and I had a desk and paper to write to my folks if I wanted.”

“I met some of the other girls who were staying there and we were all in the same situation. We hung out a lot, talking and telling each other our stories of how we got there.”

“My roommate was from a wealthy family in Oklahoma. I don’t remember what she said father did, but it had something to do with oil. Her name was Florence and she was very nice to me. She asked me to call her Flo and she told me that her parents had sent her to a private school in Chicago because they wanted her to get a better education. She started to skip classes and hang out with the wrong crowd in the school. There were a few local girls there on scholarship that she became friendly with. The local girls brought in liquor for some of the dormitory girls so they could party with them after classes in their rooms.”

“Flo told to me she started to drink and use uppers at the exclusive boarding school. One night she told me that she was getting horny and had sex with one of the other rich girls at the school. Then she started to sneak out and went to some parties in the neighborhood with a few of the local girls who went to the school. That’s when she got knocked up and sent to Florida to have the baby.”

“She used to go to sex parties where the girls and boys drank and smoked weed and they also slept with anyone who was there. She said they had a lot of orgy parties and she did a lot of kinky sex with the girls that were there. I was shocked as I never heard of anything like that. I guess I really lived a sheltered life back then” Dawn told them.

"As the weeks past I was getting a bigger stomach and also homesick. I was down in the dumps and one night Flo asked me why I was so glum? I told her I missed my folks and Marcus; and she came over to me and started to stroke my hair. Then she kissed me softly on the back of my neck. And before I realized it we were making out on her bed."

"So did you do it with her?" Amanda blurted out.

"Kind of, we just kissed and touched each other, but that was all. I really started to like being with Flo. I guess it was just someone to hold me and care about me at that moment. I felt wanted when I was with her. She was also a lot of fun; with her sense of humor during the day time when the other girls were there too, and I miss her sometimes" Dawn answered.

"Giving birth there wasn't so bad. The problem is…" she paused to reflect on what she was going to say; "I gave birth to a little boy, just like my mom…." She paused again, this time a bit longer. "But my son was born on Christmas Day…and I named him Christopher." The tears started to flow down Dawn's cheeks in a torrent but she continued talking, but much slower.

"I kissed his cheeks and held him in my arms for a few minutes after he was born…, then the nurse took him away and I never saw him again."

"Every year when Christmas comes around" she stopped talking and sat silently for a moment, "I get very depressed and can't stop crying. Even though I eventually got married and had more children, that day hurts. It really hurts" Dawn said as tears streamed down her cheeks, soaking the tissue she was holding in her hand. Crying now, she said through her tears "I miss my son so much. It still hurts me that I was forced to give him up…and never saw or touched him again."

The others in the room were also moved, and there wasn't a dry eye in the room, even Doctor Willentz started to tear up.

"Let's take a quick break" Doctor Willentz said as he stood up to stretch his legs and took a deep breath as he turned away from the group.

Amanda came over to Dawn and put her arm around her shoulder trying to comfort her. Dawn stood up and embraced her and cried softly on her shoulder for a while. Trying to compose herself, she thanked Amanda for her feelings of compassion.

Jose walked over to the window and looked out, drying his eyes with his sleeve.

After a few minutes a nurse brought in the lunch cart everyone took a tray and sat down silently at a long table in a corner of the room. It was near a large window that overlooked a small treed preserve in the hills of Bergen County, near the Palisades.

The food was not bad and everyone finished most of what was on their tray. Non caffeinated fruit drinks were served along with decaf coffee and a small piece of lemon sponge cake.

After lunch Doctor Willentz called everyone back to the circle and asked Dawn if she felt she was able to continue her story.

"Yes, I can" she said. "After I gave birth" she continued, "the boarding school had me stay another week to recuperate from the birth and then they drove me to the airport. I flew back home right after New Year's Day that year."

"I was now almost sixteen, had sex once, had a baby I was forced to give away, was sent to Florida for six months. And my parents expected me to return to Maplewood High School as if nothing had happened. I didn't know how I was going to do it; but I did!" Dawn said with conviction after realizing what she had overcome at that point in her life.

"So when I went to school that first day my best friend Annette Marie came with me. She gave me the encouragement I needed to make it through that day. She was the only one other than my family who knew everything that happened to me."

"Returning to school was better than I thought it would be. I was only one semester behind my friends at this point, but that worked out for the best. The younger kids in my classes didn't know me and I went from class to class apprehensive and fearful of being taunted. But nothing happened and no one had said anything to me. I guess they really didn't know or realize that I was gone for six months. My family apparently never told anyone about my pregnancy so I felt better after that day."

"My oldest sister was in college already and my dad was working at night to make a little extra money to help pay for her tuition at Rutgers. She had a partial scholarship but it was still very hard for my dad to make ends meet at home."

"My next oldest sister had graduated from high school that past June and was working at a community college to help pay for her tuition. That was the only way she would be able to go to college. My dad insisted that all his daughters get an education so they would not be dependent on a man to support them."

"Funny, though, he never let my mother go to work. He didn't want his friends to think he could not support a family. That was too bad. My mom was an avid reader and before they were married she was a secretary to a big Wall Street executive at the New York Stock Exchange. But after their wedding my dad insisted she stop working. So she went to church every morning, smoked a pack of cigarettes a day, and read a new book almost every other night. That was her life."

"To help out the family I started to work part time after school at a bakery in town. The pay was okay for a kid and I got to bring home the left over bread and cakes at the end of the day before they went stale. I worked there until I graduated high school and then I applied for a receptionist position. I really had no interest in college. I just wanted to make a few bucks and I hoped I would meet someone along the way to marry" as Dawn continued with her life story.

"There was a sign on Route 3 I passed while driving with my sister that said 'help wanted'. The next day I had her drop me off and I went in and applied for a job. I had no idea what the position was for and I really didn't care. I just needed a better paying job than the bakery paid me. I found out it was a back office clerical position for some large company in Clifton. I was interviewed and I accepted the position when they offered it to me. The money was a lot better than the bakery so I thought I was doing well."

"The problem was I had to dress nicely for the office and all I had was one or two church outfits. I couldn't go to work in jeans. My mom didn't have any extra money to buy me a new blouse or two so I wore the same two church outfits for two weeks until I got my first pay check. The older ladies that worked there were very nice to me and didn't say anything about my clothes to embarrass me. Then I went to the mall and bought as much clothing as my first paycheck would allow me to buy."

"I was the youngest girl there. Most of the people there were more mature women who were either married or divorced. I got along with them and didn't have any problems. My supervisor was an older middle aged man named William. He sat in a corner office with windows on two sides, at the end of the floor near the elevator. He would come over to my desk a lot during the day and sit down in my cubicle and start some small talk with me."

"At first I just thought he was being nice to me as I was the new girl in the office. Then after a week or so of the same thing I started to realize that he was interested in more than small talk with me. He asked me out for lunch one day and I told him I didn't know if I could as what would the other ladies in the office say?"

"He replied that he didn't think they would care one bit. They were either married, or divorced and looking elsewhere for a man. So I went to lunch with him. I was eighteen, what did I know?"

"William was a perfect gentleman. He told me his wife and child had died in childbirth a few years ago and he only recently thought about dating again. He said that I had a kind face and he liked talking to me. I guess he didn't feel I was above him; some of the divorced women in the office were real lookers, if you understand what I am saying."

"So I stated to date William on a steady basis. He was in his early forties, decent looking, and I had just turned eighteen. We would go out after work for dinner or go dancing afterwards. He never picked me up at home as I was sure my parents would object due to our age difference. But he made me feel good about myself. He paid attention to me and no one had ever really done that before, except for Marcus."

"It was about two weeks after we were dating that he asked me back to his apartment right after work. It was really nice. There was a doorman at the front entrance and it was located on a cliff looking out at Manhattan. That night we ate in. He had some Chinese food delivered and he opened a bottle of Saki for us to drink with dinner."

"I never drank wine, or Saki, before and I think I drank more than I should have. The sun had set and he put on some soft music. William turned the lights way down, almost off, as we looked out at the Manhattan skyline while sitting on his sofa. I know I got tipsy from the Saki and a little silly also. He laughed and took me in his arms, and we kissed for the first time. The glittering night lights of Manhattan were just across the Hudson River; and I felt like I was in a dream world. His arms surrounded me; he held me securely, protecting me from the world and his kisses were so soft, yet filled with passion. I submitted to his needs" she paused, "all his needs, and I really enjoyed it. We had gone into his bedroom and I never had sex with a man like that in a bed before. He was very intense, yet gentle, with me and I had multiple orgasms. I only did it once before, with Marcus in the back seat of his car, and I wasn't turned on like what William did to me. This was a cool new experience for me."

"I stayed over that night in his bed and the next morning he drove me to work with him. When we walked in some of the women stared at me but they didn't say a word. I didn't realize I was wearing the same outfit as I did yesterday until Josephine, my so called friend in the next cubicle, asked if I went home to change last night. That was when I realized how I was dressed. But at that point there was nothing I could do about it. Plus my car was left in the parking lot overnight and both William and I walked in together the next morning. From then on I had a spare outfit in my car just in case."

"When I was in Florida they taught us about birth control and how to use condoms and other devices. Luckily it wasn't a Catholic charity or I would have become pregnant again before I got married. I made sure William used protection that night before we did it. I may not be the brightest, but I'm not totally stupid either."

"After six months of dating William asked me to marry him. I immediately said yes and he got me a huge diamond ring. It was almost one carat with two smaller diamonds on each side. I flipped out when he gave it to me. I was so happy I couldn't wait to call Annette Marie and tell her."

Amanda asked how he proposed to her and Dawn told them how he did it.

"William waited until dinner time when it was dark and the Manhattan skyline was all lit up. Then he knelt down on one knee and asked me to marry him. I was so excited I couldn't stop jumping up and down and screaming with excitement. The next day I went into the office and showed the ring to the women I worked with. They congratulated me and said I was lucky to be marrying the boss. I said I know, he is a great supervisor, and they all looked at me kind of funny."

"Don't you know" one of the ladies asked me, "he owns the company" she said to me.

"I had no idea" Dawn said to the group. "He never mentioned it and I never asked. I assumed he was just the supervisor and did well. He was the one who interviewed me for the job and hired me on the spot. Go know!"

Dawn continued saying "now I had to tell my parents I was engaged to a man who was about my father's age. They never met him or even knew I was dating. When I didn't come home some nights I said I was at Annette's. As my best friend she knew about William and kept my secret. That's what best friends do for one another."

Shaniqua interrupted and asked "how did you tell them"?

Dawn thought for a moment, trying to remember exactly how she did bring the subject up to them. Then she told the group how she introduced William to her family.

"I asked William one night if I could borrow his car on Sunday so I could go home with it early the next morning. I pulled up to my parent's house, parked the car in front, and I sat there and waited for my parents to leave for church. When they opened the front door and saw me sitting in a metallic red Cadillac convertible with a white top and red leather seats their jaws dropped. My mother ran out of the house and over to me and quickly asked if I was doing something illegal."

"I didn't answer her with words. I just lifted my left hand up and showed her my diamond engagement ring. I told her I was getting married to a great guy and I was very happy. I was over eighteen and they couldn't stop me even if they wanted to."

"My mom asked if I loved him, and I said yes."

"Well" my mom said, "that's good enough for me. I will speak to the priest and we'll set a date."

"She realized there was nothing she could do to stop me as I wasn't home a lot anyway. I guess she correctly assumed I was sleeping out with somebody."

"My father peered over my mom's shoulder when I showed her the ring, and he said "nice car."

"And that was about it. We had a small church wedding that my mom and I planned and then I moved into William's apartment full time after our honeymoon."

"There was a local bar that my dad used to hang out in after work and they had a large back room that they had affairs in; weddings and sweet sixteens, that kind of stuff."

Jose turned his head and looked over at her and asked where she went for her honeymoon? He was very inquisitive that day because he was usually not a conversationalist.

"Oh, we went to Puerto Rico. We stayed at a great hotel near San Juan that had its own private beach. One night William and I did it on our balcony after dark. I heard the waves crashing onto the beach below us as I was bent over holding onto the railing and facing the ocean while he had sex with me from behind. I thought it was very romantic."

Jose interrupted her "I was born in Puerto Rico" he said. "I go back once a year to see my mother. It's a beautiful island, isn't it?" he asked.

"Yes it is" Dawn responded to him. Then she continued talking about her honeymoon.

"We took tours all over the island and one morning we flew over to St. Thomas to go shopping" she told the group. "William said it's duty free there, and he bought a Rolex watch for a few thousand dollars less than it would cost here in the states."

"We also bought a lot of expensive liquor that we were able to bring back with us duty free. At that time I had to rely on what William knew about booze. Now I can drink him under the table. That's also why I'm here in the institute" Dawn told them.

"When we left Puerto Rico and flew back to New Jersey we settled into his apartment on the Palisades. It was great since then we both went to work together in the morning. That lasted for a few months until I got pregnant with our first child. We had decided that it was time to have a family so we started trying. I must be a fertile Myrtle because I got pregnant almost immediately."

"Due to the pregnancy I could only work part time and I usually left early to beat the traffic."

"I had the normal throwing up and other symptoms like I had the last time I was pregnant, but the end result was worth it. I gave birth to a little boy. "

"We named him Richard. William thought that was a strong masculine name and I liked it also. So when we brought Richard home from the hospital I stopped working and took care of the baby full time."

"In the next few years I got pregnant twice more and we had a girl each time. The apartment was too small for all those kids and it was very crowded. William decided that it was time to move to a bigger place."

"He called this broker he knew and very quickly he was able to sell his condo apartment. The broker found a much larger one for us and we moved to a multi floored condo in the building next to ours. It was perfect as I already knew the neighborhood and the side roads in town. The new condo had more bedrooms and had a very nice view of Manhattan just like the old one did."

"But we didn't spend as much time romancing as we did before the kids. Either one of the kids always woke up and called to us or someone always needed something, a bottle or a diaper change. It was the same routine every day."

"As a stay at home mom I enjoyed it in the beginning, but then it got tiresome. Most of my friends were still single, and with three kids under five they are a lot to handle, and I was always tired and lonely. I guess I was bored to a certain extent too."

"One day I met this good looking lady in the elevator who was dressed very smartly and we started to talk as we walked into the lobby. It was just small talk, really about nothing much. She said her name was Kathy and she was usually home during the day and worked at night. I didn't give it much thought at the moment. But in the next few weeks I started to see her more and more."

"Then on a Wednesday I think it was, when my mom was babysitting so I could go food shopping, I met her at the supermarket. Mom usually helped me out on Wednesdays so I could go out food shopping. So when I bumped into Kathy that day she asked me how I was doing and if I needed anything to please call her. She reminded me that she was almost always home during the day time. I told her how bored I was staying home and the kids were a handful. She gave me her business card with her phone number on it. I didn't look at it then but thanked her and put the card in my coat pocket. I felt I should at least be courteous so I gave her my cell number in exchange."

"Two days later Kathy called me and asked if I needed some baby sitters during the day. She said she was a movie producer and needed a younger girl for a one time shoot in a movie. They were doing it in her apartment to save production costs and the girl they had hired couldn't make it that day. She said the whole production company was there and they needed a girl immediately for an hour or two. And she would have two script girls watch the kids in her bedroom while I worked in her apartment on the movie. I didn't know what to expect, but I said yes. It sounded exciting and a break from the daily boredom of a housewife. So I grabbed all the babies and went up to the penthouse floor. That was where she lived."

"I was never up that high and the views were spectacular. Her apartment was really sharp. She told me a designer from the city had just finished it last week. She had light pink carpet with the most comfortable matching leather sofas I had ever sat in. I didn't know they made things like that; they were so soft and plush. Then I saw there were movie lights set up all over the apartment on tripods and a lot of people walking around. There was also a table set up with a dozen different foods on platters that anyone could just walk over to it and eat. She thanked me for coming and said I could make two thousand dollars cash for one to two hours of work. It sounded good as William never gave me my own money. I had a credit card but it only had a small credit limit on it. I told Kathy yes and I was excited to be in a real movie, but I was really very nervous about it too."

"I was honest and told her I had never acted before and I didn't want to ruin her movie."

"She explained that all I had to do was act naturally, relax and have a good time. I wasn't sure what I had to do but when we walked into the master bedroom there was this great looking young man standing there, totally naked."

"Kathy introduced me to Chad. She said that was his stage name. He was very good looking with a full head of wavy brown hair, gray eyes like a wolf's, and his muscles were awesome; and he was really long, if you know what I mean. I had only been with Marcus and William and I never imagined it could be that big. I knew at that moment what I was going to do in the movie; and I said to myself the hell with it… and I did it."

"William was just over fifty now and closing in on sixty in a few more years and his sex drive was not what I needed. And this movie thing immediately looked like I would enjoy it".

"Kathy had a young costume lady get me an outfit to wear and another did my makeup. This young looking boy who was also in the apartment was a hair dresser and he did my hair. In just under thirty minutes I was ready for the movie. I never looked so good. I didn't recognize myself in the mirror when he was done."

"Kathy told me to slowly walk in to the room, smile, and Chad would lead me into the scene. I was to go with the flow. She said there would be minimal dialogue to say."

"Chad took me I in his arms and started to slowly undress me. He unbuttoned my blouse, unhooded my bra and he started to leisurely lick and kiss my neck. To be honest with you it really felt good."

"Slowly he slid his face downwards to my chest, licking and sucking on my erect nipples. There was a small fan in the corner and the breeze caused them to stand up. Then he leisurely moved his head even lower, his tongue licking my abdomen very gently. I don't think I have to tell you the rest" Dawn said to the group.

"Yes you do" Mei chirped in. "You can't leave us hanging."

"Okay" Dawn said. "He moved down to between my legs with his tongue and I couldn't stand anymore I was so excited and wet."

"He was also great in bed" Dawn squealed with delight just thinking about him.

"I spent two hours the first day in bed with him. We did everything and we did it everywhere in the apartment. I did things I never knew my body could do. I didn't want it to stop. I couldn't help myself. My body just had multiple orgasms one after the other that I couldn't control. I just loved it" Dawn continued. "And I was completely exhausted when it was finally over. I never felt the warm sweat of a man's body before on my face or body as when I was doing that movie. We were both really going at it and our bodies were wet and slippery. I had a hard time holding on to him as he furiously pushed into me very rapidly."

“When we were finally finished I collapsed on the bed and didn’t move for almost five minutes just trying to catch my breath. I really enjoyed that afternoon.”

“I was paid two thousand dollars in cash that day. I never had that much money or fun in my life at one time. I thanked Kathy and said anytime she needed me again to just call. I definitely wanted to do it again.”

The group sat there in amazement. Mousey Dawn was becoming a porn star. They couldn’t believe it.

“It didn’t take Kathy long to call me back” Dawn continued, “and this became a steady thing. Every few weeks she did a movie in her place and she had baby sitters there to handle the kids. She even turned one of her smaller bedrooms into a playroom for my kids. She hired a professional nanny and a helper for her and she even outfitted the room with age appropriate toys for the kids.”

“On one shoot she had two very pretty girls there who joined me in a swap session with two other guys. It was a six person scene and going well until I realized I was having oral sex with one of the girls, and enjoying it! After that I became bisexual and also had sex with girls on the set.”

“I see no difference to be honest with you. Skin is skin and if I get turned on I really don’t care who does it” Dawn stated matter of factly.

“The only problem was that after a movie was finished I went home and had a shot of really expensive whisky that William had in a locked wooden liquor cabinet. I usually collapsed on my sofa with the drink to try to settle my nerves down and relax. I really enjoyed working for Kathy” Dawn said with some enthusiasm. “But I needed to come down from my emotional high and the drinking helped me to unwind.”

"The men she hired were all young and really built. A few times Chad called to meet me when there was no movie being made. I guess I was really good in bed."

The group sat motionless and looked at her in amazement. Dawn just did not seem like the type to be a porn star. She wasn't flashy or big chested either.

"Once when he came to my apartment he brought along a teenage girl who was about seventeen as a baby sitter. Chad and I had a good time in my apartment while the baby sitter took the kids out for a long walk on the paths in the nearby park. The young girl was a brunette with huge boobs and a small tush and she was wearing very tight jeans that outlined her body."

"Once when she was there and all the kids were napping the baby sitter joined us too. That's when we really started to have threesomes off the set as a continuing thing. A short while after that it moved to the movie set and soon I was screwing both men and women in the movies; and at home on the side as a steady thing, plus my alcohol intake also increased."

"After one movie session in the morning the crew stopped for lunch. I was really tired because I was up with the kids during the night and I just had a scene with two men that lasted for almost three hours. I was exhausted. Kathy said she had a pill that would give me energy for the afternoon shoot and I took it. She said it was Adderall and it was a legal pill and not like cocaine or stuff. So I swallowed it and that is what started my drug use. She would always get it for me when I needed it. Whenever I took it my sexual desires and energy increased. Kathy said it was an aphrodisiac. "

"My mom helped me out as much as she could at the other times when I wasn't making a movie. She never knew what I was doing for extra cash; she just assumed William gave money to me. But as time went on she was getting older and wasn't feeling well; and she stopped coming as often as she used to."

"Being alone when the kids were napping, and no one was screwing me in the afternoon, I started to regularly take a shot of scotch or two to relax a bit and pass the time of day. But my drinking increased to the point where I was downing a bottle every three days. Then it went to two days, and finally when I was drinking a bottle a day I couldn't hide it anymore from William. Between my booze and uppers I was a mess."

"The kids were not being cared for properly. I forgot to change their diapers, or feed them, or even bath them at night. All I wanted to do was drink, pop pills, screw and sleep. I stopped eating and got even thinner, and I was very thin to start with! The thought of food repulsed me. My weight kept dropping and I started to look in the mirror and see myself as fat."

"It's not that I don't love William, I do. But I felt lonely and not wanted. He was working a lot trying to expand and grow his company. Plus he is much older than me and I wanted more sex than he was giving me, or even wanted to give me. And the extra movie sex was really exciting when I did it. But when it slowed down and the movie was over, I bottomed out."

"That's when it all came crashing down. William came home one night and found me passed out on the floor with an empty bottle next to me. I used to hide it pretty good but that one afternoon I really got plastered. I was drinking all day and before he came home from work I must have gone blank and hit the floor. "

"When he saw me with the empty bottle in my hand on the floor he stood there and he knew. He then realized I was an alcoholic and called a friend of his who was an ex alcoholic. His pal knew what Doctor Willentz did here at the institute and he recommended Doctor Willentz to William. But William doesn't know anything about my pill taking. So William brought me here, and here I am!"

"And I never told William about my extra income activities either. If he ever found out he would divorce me. He's kind of straight laced that way, I guess."

"Dawn, how do you think you can deal with your issues?" Doctor Willentz asked her.

"I know that I have to go to a twelve step program for my drinking and drugs" she answered. "But I don't know if I can give up the extra sex with Chad and the movie stuff" she continued.

Doctor Willentz told her "right now you have to concentrate on your addiction; the sex is really a marital problem that you have to come to terms with. I can't advise you to continue or stop. But I can tell you that if it is the root cause of your addictions then you have to face your sex problem head on and either stop the adultery and movies or have William agree to you making these kinds of films. That is going to be your biggest problem."

Doctor Willentz continued "and Dawn you have anorexic issues too. We are going to also try to work on them privately while you are in here. If we run out of time I know of a clinic near your home that I can recommend you to go to."

"Before we break for lunch" Doctor Willentz said to Dawn, "I want you to think about your issues with your self-image. You think you are not pretty or wanted by men but apparently there are plenty of men who think you are. And the fact that you are now starring in porn movies, though I cannot judge you on that, it has to play in to your value system of self-worth as a positive rather than a negative influence. Do you really think you have to do that to reaffirm your self- worth? I don't think you have to, but that is for you to come to terms with."

The doctor continued "I want to thank Mei and Dawn for sharing their backgrounds with us and tomorrow we will hear from Juan in the morning session. Please go back to your rooms and dinner will be ready in an hour or so. I will see everyone at dinner."

Chapter Four – Evening

Everyone went back to the sun room in the wing where they were staying.

The Willentz Institute is situated in an old turn of the century mansion in Northwestern Bergen County in New Jersey. It was donated by a wealthy patient of Doctor Willentz a few years ago. The woman's family had been in the real estate business in New Jersey and when she had some severe emotional problems her family paid for her therapy as a private patient with Doctor Willentz.

She in turn was so grateful to him for giving her life back to her that she bought, renovated and donated the mansion to his newly formed foundation. She did this with an inheritance she had received from her late grandfather who had been a very successful two family home developer in Bayonne New Jersey.

Amanda stayed in the sun room and watched television while Shaniqua went to the public phone and called her office at work.

Barbara was hungry, excused herself from the rest, and waked slowly but steadily over to the snack machine and bought three chocolate covered whole wheat bars to satisfy her cravings till dinner was brought out.

Mei and Dawn were talking to each other and as they walked down the hall Mei asked her if she would like to sit by a window and talk a little more with her. "Of course I would" Dawn answered. "We probably have a lot in common" she continued, as they went to the big picture window and looked out at the cows grazing on the rolling green field of the farm next door to the institute.

They both pulled up chairs and sat down close to each other so their conversation would not be overheard.

Dawn told her that she did not consider what she did prostitution as she was being paid to be in a movie. That, in her mind, was different. She wasn't really being paid for sex, but to act in a movie. The sex, she thought, was just an extra bonus that she thoroughly enjoyed. It was just part of the movie; you know, the job, work, sort of.

But Mei knew what it really was. She had many years of experience doing what Dawn did. Mei knew that getting paid money for sex was prostitution. Whether you were in a movie or not, if you got paid for it, then there is no two ways around it. But she did not tell her that. She did not want to hurt Dawns feelings. Mei sensed that Dawn was mentally fragile after hearing her story and felt truly sorry for her.

"I'm glad I met you" Dawn said. "I don't feel so alone here now."

"I agree" Mei responded quietly. "I guess it can be very lonely here, talking about yourself to strangers."

"Yer" Dawn answered. "I don't know much about this therapy stuff here but I really have no choice. I don't want to lose my husband and kids. I miss them already. I have to stay here and try to recover."

"Well if you ever need to talk some more privately, my room is next to yours" Mei told her.

As Mei said that she gently pulled her hospital gown up slightly over her knees as she picked up her legs to tuck them under and sit on them, on the leather lounge chair. Her tanned thigh was showing and a little of her cheeks were peeking out from under the hospital gown. Not enough to get in trouble but enough to send a message to Dawn.

As Mei tucked her legs under her, Dawn saw the gown go up and got the message. Dawn smiled and said "maybe if I have to talk some more tonight I just might stop by."

Mei smiled and said "I look forward to that."

It was now after five and the ward nurse walked in and asked everyone to please follow her to the dining room for dinner. They all got up and as they walked down the hall they could smell the food cooking downstairs in the kitchen.

The mansion was very stately. As they walked to dinner some of them took the small elevator down to the main floor hallway, while the others walked down the wide curving center stairway into the main hall. It was then, at the bottom of the stairs, that they first noticed the stained dark wood paneling and the pictures of a rural country side. There were horse pictures on one wall and a very large pastoral scene of a farm on the facing wall.

This floor was very different than the new wing that was built on in the rear of the mansion where their ward is. This looked like old money as their ward was a modern hospital like ward with rooms lined up and a nurse's desk around a corner at the front entry.

As they entered Doctor Willentz stood up and greeted them individually and asked them to please sit wherever they liked. The table was very large and he sat in the middle so as to be able to talk intimately to everyone during dinner.

Two women in white uniforms brought out a stainless steel cart filled with fresh fruit cups to start the meal.

Everyone picked up a small spoon to eat with. Dawn never had anything like this when she was growing up so she waited to see which utensil everyone was using. Her first impulse was a small fork that was on her napkin, but she hesitated and watched Doctor Willentz and when he used a small spoon, she picked up hers.

After the fruit cup was removed a cart with soup was wheeled in. Everyone was given a choice of chicken soup with dumplings or split pea soup with garlic croutons. Most of them took the chicken soup as they really never had split pea soup before.

"I love split pea soup" Jose announced to everyone. "When I was a waiter in Manhattan they made fresh pea soup every Thursday, with croutons too."

Dawn took her slippers off under table, and as Mei was sitting next to her, she started to stroke Mei's foot with hers.

Mei smiled and continued eating her fruit cup.

After a few minutes another food cart was wheeled out and it had plates of roasted organic chicken with pan fried small white potatoes and glazed onions over fresh French cut green beans covered with oregano.

"Hey" Jose called out, "this is the first time I ever ate anything without ketchup. It really tastes great."

They all looked at him and started to quietly laugh.

Barbara finally said something, "I never use ketchup because it takes away the taste from the food."

No one answered her but they thought to themselves "no wonder you are the size you are".

Doctor Willentz said "eating without ketchup is probably the best way to eat. It allows you to actually taste the food. It's not hidden under a sweet tomato and sugar coating".

When they were finished eating a staffer brought the desert cart out. It was over whelming and on it were assorted butter glazed cheese Danish stacked high and large chocolate chip cookies on the other serving dish. The staffer also asked each person if they wanted decaf coffee or tea.

After desert they were escorted back to the second floor rear ward where their rooms were supervised by a staff nurse.

Everyone had a small television in their room. There was also a larger one in the sun room with lounge chairs where they could sit together and watch the news or whatever else the nurse put on the television.

Some of them went to their room to read and relax and a few stayed to watch television with the others.

The door on the rooms was supposed to be kept somewhat open at all times during the day unless it was a medical emergency. At night they were allowed to close them.

Barbara went into her room to by herself read the local newspaper that was delivered every morning and Shaniqua went into her room and turned on her television to watch and relax.

Jose and Amanda stayed in the sun room constantly changing the channels until they both decided on something to watch.

Mei and Dawn excused themselves and went into the ladies room. Once inside they closed the door and embraced each other.

Grinding their bodies together and passionately kissing with their tongues dashing in and out of each other's mouths, they started to grope each other's bodies. As they were masturbating each other with their hands pushed under the hospital gowns, they had to stop when they realized they were starting to make uncontrollable throaty moaning sounds, very guttural sounding.

Mei did not want to stop and she took Dawn into one of the larger handicapped stalls and had her sit down on the toilet. She knelt in front of her and lifted up Dawn's gown. She started to lick Dawn in a darting motion until Dawn started to have an orgasm. Dawn struggled to keep quiet and did not make any loud sounds, and she enjoyed every moment as her body strained from the passion. Finally Mei stopped and she stood up and changed places with Dawn. When Mei was fully satisfied they both stood up and opened the stall door. They embraced with soft yet passionate kisses. Hugging each other and gently kissing on each other's neck they embraced with warmth and passion again. Finally they pulled themselves apart, kissed one last time, then washed up and left the ladies room together to go their own rooms to rest.

The rest of the night was uneventful for everyone.

The nurse at the head desk by the door turned the lights down in the ward and it was time for everyone to go to sleep.

Chapter Four – Day Two - Juan

It was six thirty in the morning and the sun was shining through the windows. The floor nurse came around waking everybody up who did not get out of bed when the lights went on.

They all staggered into their individual bathrooms and the showers started.

Afterwards they all met in the sun room and started to go downstairs together for breakfast.

This time they all waited for the small elevator. Being in a strange bed was not restful for most of them. Bleary eyed they took turns getting on the elevator until finally everyone was in the dining room and seated. Dawn and Mei waited until they were the last ones on the elevator by themselves. They kissed good morning when the doors closed and held hands until the doors opened on the ground floor and they walked together to the table to sit next to each other.

When everyone sat down for breakfast they had their choice of orange or grapefruit juice.

Then there was a small breakfast buffet set up on a small side table and they all took their plates and went to get their food.

Scrambled eggs glistening under the heat lamps, small diced potatoes with onions, bits of red peppers, a tray full of crisp hickory smoked bacon, buttery breakfast rolls, milk and assorted cold cereals were there for them to take as they pleased.

As they sat down Doctor Willentz walked in and joined them for breakfast.

"How did everyone sleep last night?" Doctor Willentz asked.

They all nodded their heads and a few mumbled "okay".

"Good" he said. "After breakfast we'll go right upstairs and begin our morning session where we left off".

Mei was sitting next to Dawn again and as she put her right arm down towards her seat she paced her hand on Dawns upper thigh.

Both women smiled, yet did not look at each other. They just continued eating as if nothing was happening.

Barbara was still hungry so she got up for a second helping of eggs and potatoes.

Shaniqua and Amanda had the cold cereal with milk and Jose just had coffee and some small Danish for breakfast.

Shaniqua asked why they couldn't be in their street clothes and had to stay in the hospital gowns and robes.

Doctor Willentz explained that if everyone was dressed the same it kind of broke down barriers and everyone was equal. It just made it easier for everyone to relate to each other.

No one knew if that was true or not but it made sense to them.

So nobody else questioned it and when they all finished their food they gathered together and went back to the elevator to go upstairs.

Doctor Willentz led them back into the sun room where the lounge chairs were set up in a circle again, and they all sat down to start the morning session.

"Juan" Doctor Willentz said, "Would you please tell us something about yourself this morning"?

"Well, I was born in Puerto Rico and after I was two years old my mother moved to New York."

"I don't remember my father at all. My mother said he ran away with another woman and I have never spoken to him in my whole life. I was raised by my mother and my older sisters in an apartment in the South Bronx. Two years ago my mother moved back to Puerto Rico to be with her other sisters and brothers."

"It really wasn't too bad in the South Bronx. I didn't know any better then and there was a lot of love in the house".

"My mother worked in a sewing factory six days a week and my two older sisters while in high school worked in local stores to help us survive."

"They were all paid in cash so no taxes were ever taken out. We were citizens because we were born in Puerto Rico but for some reason they never tried to get a better paying job. I never could understand that."

"We were on welfare and food stamps so maybe that would be the reason; I don't honestly know. But when my sisters graduated high school only one of them, Marta, decided to go to a local college. It was a two year college and she was doing okay. The career counselor at the school sat down with her and they decided she should try to get into a nursing school when she finished there. So that is what she did."

"Marta is now a surgical nurse at a big hospital in the Bronx. She used to come home and tell us about all the shootings, stabbings and weird surgeries that happened there that she worked on with the doctors. To be honest it was hard to hear those stories. A lot of blood and guts stuff."

"Marta said the head of surgery told her it was almost worse than Viet Nam when he was serving there."

"People have no respect for human life in the Bronx. That's what I think" said Jose.

Amanda, being curious, interrupted and asked "what kind of unusual operations did she watch?"

"I remember" Jose said, "her telling me that once they had to operate on a young girl who was raped and then stabbed. She was only eleven and her intestines were hanging out of her abdomen. She assisted as they opened her up and had to cut off yards of intestine that was too far cut to be re-stitched."

"The police had to guard her in her ward because the rapist told her he was coming back for her to finish the job. He was going to kill her but was interrupted by neighbors who were throwing out their garbage in the rear yard dumpster. A few months later the girl came back in for an abortion. She was pregnant from the rapist and her family did not want the baby born. They said it was a disgrace to the family."

"Wow," said Amanda. "That's amazing."

"Then once she had to assist a rectal surgeon who operated on a man who had glass stuck in his ass. Marta said he was gay and he was having kinky sex with a new lover when the bottle broke. Look, I'm bisexual but I know better than to stick glass up my ass" Jose said.

Doctor Willentz interjected and asked that he move on with his story.

"Okay. As I said I have two older sisters. They really took care of me most of the time as my mother was working. They thought of me as a doll. When I was a little kid and my mother wasn't home they used to dress me up in their old little girls clothes and put lip stick on me. They thought I was so cute that I should have been a girl."

"But that all ended when my mother took in a boyfriend. His name was Ramon and he was not too bad a guy. He was very quiet and reserved. But he didn't like when my sisters dressed me like a girl, so they stopped. Although he was a pretty quiet man, he was a little macho that way."

"Ramon worked in the city for the health department doing paper work and with his income and health benefits my mother only had to work one job. That's when my mother really took over the house. My older sisters were basically out of the house by then and that's when I came to know my mother really well."

"My grandmother also lived with us for a while and we used to call her Senora Presidenta. She ruled our house with an iron fist. That is until my mother started to stay home more. But she always had an opinion and my mother listened. But she didn't always agree and do what she said. Thank God."

Amanda interrupted and confirmed "so you were raised in an all-female house Jose?"

"Yes, when I was smaller" he answered. "But I didn't know I liked boys until I was about thirteen. Actually I like girls too" he said to everyone.

"I guess you can call me bisexual."

"Anyway I grew up in the South Bronx and went to high school there. There were plenty of fights and gang shit going on but I stayed away from it all. I didn't hang out with them and I went right back home when school was over."

"There was this one kid who was always in fights. He was a white kid with flaming red hair. Actually he was the only white kid in the school and he was always getting into fights. I used to take the bus home with him and we would sometimes talk. I asked him why he was always getting into fights."

"He told me that he started the fights so they would leave him alone. He had a reputation of being crazy. But he was really a very bright guy. I guess it was his way of self-preservation."

"So anyway one day after gym class I was in the shower when this kid named Julio was standing next to me and we started to talk about nothing special. He said I looked good naked. I told him he did too. He had his hair brushed back and he had very chiseled facial features. I couldn't take my eyes off of him. "

"After the shower we both got dressed and he asked me if I wanted to come to his apartment after school to watch some television and maybe play some ball. I said okay and we walked to his home when school let out."

"His parents were still working and he had the key to get in. We both entered his apartment and walked into the living room when he said turned to me and said that the shower was fun and we both should get naked again. I thought why not, and we both got undressed."

"He stepped towards me and started to play with my genitals and kiss me on the lips. It felt good and not weird, so I did the same to him. I guess that was when I started my gay life, so to speak."

Shaniqua spoke up and asked "how long did you stay with him?"

"We remained close through high school. When I started to work we kind of lost track of each other; and he went away to college. I got a job in the hospital doing janitorial stuff; the one where my sister Marta worked. It wasn't a bad job either. She got me that job there. She was dating the HR director and as a favor to her I was hired. Of course it didn't hurt that he was married to an old hag and Marta was twenty years younger than him. I guess blow jobs can accomplish a lot in life," Jose said.

Dawn had been sitting quietly until now. "I'm curious" she asked, "when did you start getting into girls, if you liked boys?"

"I dated some girls in high school also" he answered. "There was this one girl Maribel that was very pretty. She liked to dance and so did I. So one day I asked her to go dancing with me at a party in a friend's apartment. We had a nice time and we danced a lot together. She was a thick girl with a pretty face and short jet black hair."

"When the party started to die down, the lights were lowered and the slow music came on. We were slow dancing and she started to rub her body into mine; really it was her chest. I got turned on and then she whispered into my ear that she doesn't do anything unless she gets kissed. So I kissed her."

"Then what" Dawn excitedly asked.

"I kissed her on her lips and she opened her mouth and stuck her tongue into my mouth. Then she took my hand and led me into one of the bedrooms in the apartment. Most of the people had already left but she didn't care. She pulled me onto the bed and started to make out with me. She was the first girl I was ever with, and I let her teach me."

Dawn interjected again "Jose, did she blow you?"

"Yes, she unzipped my pants and gave me a blow job right there on the bed, on top of peoples jackets. Then she took my hand and put it under her dress and I got her off pretty quickly."

"We saw each other a lot after that. Between Julio and Maribel I had a pretty good two last years of high school. But it wasn't easy keeping each of them from knowing what I was doing with the other. They were both in my grade and we were even in a few classes together."

"After graduation Julio got a full scholarship to a college in upstate New York and Maribel got a job in a department store as a sales clerk. I didn't see Julio again until after he graduated and came back to the city to work."

"He started as an intern in a Wall Street brokerage company and was making really good money. He got his own condo on the Upper East Side and bought a BMW. He would call me and we would meet at a bar in the village and then go back to his place."

"But I only did that when Maribel was working a night shift. That retail sales job was terrible. They worked all different days and hours. Weekends too. We weren't living together yet but I was at her place almost every night when she was free. Finally she asked me if we got a place together, we could share the rent and expenses. I said okay as Julio didn't ask me to move in with him, so I said yes to her."

"I wanted to do more than clean toilets in a hospital so I had some pictures made of myself with a friend of mine and I sent them in to modeling agencies in Manhattan."

"One day I was called in and got a contract with a medium sized agency on the west side of Manhattan. They were looking for new faces because the major advertisers were just discovering that the national Latino market was worth billions of dollars. They sent me out for a lot of magazine advertising shoots and a few runways. The agency thought I was pretty and the money was really good."

"So Maribel and I decided that we had to live together to save enough money to get ahead. We finally moved into a place in Chelsea because it was convenient to both of our jobs. Plus the rent was very reasonable."

"I worked mostly in Manhattan and her department store was in midtown so she took a cross town bus together to work. Occasionally I had to do a location shoot out of town, but that was not too often."

"Everything was going great for us. We were in love and we were thinking of getting married in a year or so. She was doing okay at work and had a promotion to a department manager on the housewares floor. There was a small pay increase and really a lot of additional responsibility. But she did not mind the extra work involved and she put in the hours and effort that was needed to succeed there."

"Her department was doing better than before because she was on top of things and made sure the displays were set up right and stuff like that. Maribel instilled in her floor crew a pride that when they walked by a display if something was out of line they should straighten it up so it looked prefect."

"She won a departmental sales award from the company and they gave her another promotion to floor manager after a year of steady increases in sales. But it didn't stop there."

"The human resources person called her up to the eighth floor and asked her if she would like to go to college for management and the store would pay for it."

"What I learned much later was that she was seeing the HR manager on the on the sly. He was much older than her and married. So they had lunch time sessions in a back office on the furniture floor. The sales people never went back there for stock like they did on the clothing floors. So it was pretty much deserted and they met there continually. He thought that if he gave her something she could never get, like a college education, she would remain with him on the down low. It worked for a while too"

"She came home that night all excited and nervous. College was never an option for her as her family could never afford it. She did okay in high school and passed all the final exams and the New York State Regents too. But her mother had six children and feeding them and paying the rent came before college. So Maribel never gave it any thought."

"I told her to give it a shot, why not?"

I said "if they were going to pay for it, all she had to do was go to college and learn."

"The next day she agreed and signed up to go at night to a community college while she worked at the store during the day. The school also had summer sessions, and winter break classes too, and she took advantage of them all."

"Maribel was always studying whenever she could and graduated with honors. I remember she would get off work and rush to college. On the train she studied on her way to work, and during her lunch breaks she studied also. Her face was always in a book unless she was having sex with the HR manager."

"When she graduated from the community college she earned a great scholarship to NYU. Not only did she get the scholarship for her grades but also as a minority student and for her low income. Plus the department store picked up the rest as part of their diversity program."

"So she went to NYU at night to complete her business degree. In a few years she graduated with a degree in management and she was very proud of her accomplishment. She was the first one in her family to get a college degree. The department store then promoted her to assistant manager of corporate merchandising. Then the next step was as director of merchandising and she soon got that promotion also. There was a lot of travelling in that position. She had to go to the branch stores to oversee their displays, when they had a grand opening, and other job functions and conventions."

"It was when she went to Florida on a business trip that she met Alberto in Florida at a famous seafood restaurant in Miami. His family was from Cuba and he was the restaurant's general manager. It was a family business and was very successful. They also owned a large jewelry store in West Palm Beach. He and his brothers were highly educated and Alberto found he and Maribel had a lot in common with each other. What, I don't know; but she later told me they did."

"I believe that Maribel had mentally outgrown me and found out there was more to life than a three story walkup in Manhattan. She had stalled on the idea of marriage to me and kept coming up with excuses to put off the discussion."

"She would fly down to Miami almost every week and Alberto picked her up at the airport; and they went sailing on his boat when she was in town. He also took her out for expensive dinners, and bought her jewelry from his store that I could never afford."

"She left me a note one day last year when I came home from a photo shoot. She wrote that she had moved into a one bedroom condo Alberto bought for her on the Upper East Side. Either he flies up twice a month to be with her or she flies down to Miami the other two times. Maribel said she loves me and him, but he can provide for her better so she had to make a choice. I lost that decision."

"I was devastated. All those years I spent helping her, loving her, supporting her all meant nothing. It's not like he was better looking than me, it was a money issue. I had made good money modeling since I left the hospital job, but it started to slow down when I had a viral infection. I lost too much weight, looked too thin and the clothes just hung on me. Then photo jobs dried up. Plus Alberto lived a lifestyle in Miami that I couldn't afford in New York City, or anywhere, to be truthful."

"Feeling depressed I started to drink a little and started to think of ending it all."

"That's when I met Johnson. I was at a fashion show my agency sent me to because they needed extra models and I was their last choice. I was doing a walkway for a men's clothing company and this older man was running the show. He was the fashion director for the designer and he noticed me. Since I had lost a lot of weight I fit into the designers tightly fitted suits and my skinny butt was form fitted to the slacks."

"He came over and asked me out for dinner that night after the show was over. I accepted the invitation; mainly because it was a free meal at a five star restaurant in Manhattan and I was really hungry. So after I changed we caught a cab and rode over to midtown for dinner."

"He ordered for both of us; I really didn't care. The food at that place was fabulous and whatever he ordered I knew I was going to like. The waiter brought out lobster tails with garlic butter and paired it with a thick sirloin steak with a demi glaze and roasted red potatoes mashed with garlic and butter. The dinner was tremendous and I couldn't stop eating. When we were finally finished eating I started telling him how Maribel left me; and he made a strange suggestion to me."

"Johnson is known in the industry as a very creative person. He said I have a very pretty face and had lost a lot of weight, so why not dress in drag for the women's show he was doing next week?"

"I needed more work because I couldn't pay my bills so I said yes to the idea. I was desperate for money, but I didn't tell him that."

"He took me out shopping for under garments the next day at a sixth avenue department store. Then we went to the design studio he worked at, where he had two seamstresses fit me with a dress. I lost so much weight that I actually fit into one of the designer's dresses. It was skin tight and I looked really hot in it."

"Johnson called in his fifth avenue hair stylist to the stars and she brought a wig along for me to try on. She styled it to my face and then when they both were satisfied they had a photo shoot set up the next day for me."

"When I got to the photography studio they had me in makeup for over an hour, then the hair stylist fitted the wig on me so it fit perfectly after I got dressed."

"My picture from that photo shoot ended up on the front page of WWD since it was from a big name designer. My career was back on track again but I had to sign an exclusive contract with Johnson's company. My contract with my old agency had expired and they were just sending me out on a freelance basis. I took Johnsons offer because the money was great and they flew me to the Caribbean for some beach shots and to California also. I was having a ball. And being in warm weather place instead of a New York winter is great. "

Shaniqua interrupted again and asked "what is WWD?"

Doctor Willentz answered that "it is the fashion industry newspaper that comes out every day. Everyone in the industry reads it."

Jose then continued "the only drawback was Johnson himself. I became his love interest for the moment. I moved in with him because I couldn't afford the rent by myself; and I really didn't mind that he was in his seventies. And he really did look down on me and sometimes I felt weird being with him, but I became his newest boy toy. That annoyed me as I soon realized that I was just eye candy for him to parade around with in front of his former boyfriends on Fire Island."

"Sometimes when I was in San Francisco on a shoot and he was back in New York I dressed in drag and went to a gay bar for some relaxation, and sex. I also fooled around in New York, I couldn't help myself. As a beautiful drag queen I was in demand from the best looking guys in the bar."

"Unfortunately it all came crashing down when a picture of me was on page six in the Post kissing another man in a gay bar in New York, and Johnson saw it. He was furious and he threw me out of his condo and I was homeless again, and out of a job too."

"It was then I realized my run was over and I had hit bottom with no future ahead of me. My old agency wanted nothing to do with me as I left them for Johnson. It didn't matter that they didn't resign me on my original contract with them, although I offered to take a pay cut."

"I was depressed and I left the agency and walked down into the subway and jumped onto the tracks waiting for a train to come. Someone saw me jump and ran to the token booth to yell at the attendant to tell him to stop the train that someone was on the tracks."

"The train was coming. I heard the rattle of the steel wheels on the rails as it got louder and louder. I just stood there facing it. I closed my eyes and just waited for the impact."

"I heard it come closer and closer. The floor started to vibrate from the approaching train and I knew it would soon be over. I heard it screech as it made the tight turn in the tunnel and started to enter the station. The rush of cool air hit me in the face as it pushed the air out of the tunnel ahead of it."

"I knew that any second now my problems would soon be over. Maribel had left me, Johnson threw me out, my modeling career was in ruins, and I had nothing left to live for."

"I could hear it get closer. The sound of the steel wheels on the rails grew much more intense, I knew any second now, bam, and the end of my problems" he told everyone with resignation in his voice as it trailed off to silence.

Jose continued slowly and softly "but the train stopped about twenty feet in front of me. The police were there pretty quickly and after a short time I was in the psych ward at Bellevue. I ended up in here after Doctor Willentz came to see me."

"My mistake was I should have waited till the train was in the station and then jumped in front of it. What I did gave the conductor time to stop before hitting me."

There was silence from everyone. They listened with their emotions running on high and felt terribly sad for him. He was a genuinely nice guy and he had had a bad deal in life.

Shaniqua and Dawn were wiping the tears from their eyes after hearing his story.

Doctor Willentz asked Jose why he thought it was his fault Maribel left him. Maybe it was not him, but her mentality that caused the breakup? She wanted expensive things and maybe she never really loved him. "Maybe she used you to help support her through college?" Doctor Willentz asked him rhetorically.

"Did you ever think that she had used you while she furthered her education? It may not have mattered what you said or did. She was out for a rich guy and not everyone in the world is born into money like Alberto was. You were just a means to an end. It wasn't your fault she left you. It was just one of those things out of your control" he concluded.

This made sense to Jose and he sat there thinking about what was just said. He made no comments and sat motionless in his chair.

After a minute or so of silence Doctor Willentz said he would talk to Jose in the future about this and suggested they break for lunch.

Chapter Five – Shaniqua

The lunch cart was wheeled in with the drink cart right behind it. The usual cold lunch meats were available, plus tuna salad on rye and a delicious roasted salmon salad on a Miami onion roll with a horseradish mayonnaise lightly spread on it.

On the second cart were cold drinks plus decaf coffee and tea.

Everyone got up and they walked over to take a plate and cup and select what they were going to have for lunch.

Then they sat by the tables in the corner of the room and watched a hawk fly by with its wings spread out. It was gliding on the air current, circling the pasture below it.

Dawn and Mei sat next to each other and the others sat wherever they could, not in any particular order.

Today there was not much small talk during lunch. Everyone was thinking about how close Jose came to suicide, and it found an emotional place in each of their individual lives. It had become real to them and they internalized it.

After a half hour or so Doctor Willentz asked everyone to come back to the circle and to let Shaniqua tell her life story.

Shaniqua was a mature African-American woman in her mid-forties with close cropped hair, a caramel complexion and two tattoos on her arms. One tattoo was of a small child on her upper right bicep; and a small one with some words on her left forearm, but too small to read unless you held her forearm up to your face.

"I was born in Manhattan and raised there by my mother and father" she started by saying.

"My dad was a mailman who delivered mail in Greenwich Village for over thirty years. His route was only one square block. But there were literally hundreds of apartments in each building; and he had to sort and place their mail in their locked mail boxes in the different apartment house lobbies. He was a hardworking and a devoted family man who came home every night to his family."

"On Sundays we all went to church as a family. My mother, father, my three sisters and I never missed a Sunday service. We had on our finest clothes and afterwards we all went to a local restaurant for lunch. Dad always had a turkey platter with brown gravy and garlic mashed potatoes and whatever vegetables they had that day. He never cared for the vegetables so mom usually had one of us ate them from his plate. This went on for years and years until my father died unexpectedly."

“He was working that day delivering the mail as usual, when he went to cross the street on his lunch break to sit in the park and eat his lunch. As he was standing on the corner waiting for the light to change he had a major stroke. Dad fell to his knees and rolled over into the street. A city bus was turning the corner at that exact moment and he rolled under the rear wheels of the bus and was instantly killed.”

“My family was devastated. Mom’s life revolved around our family. Dad was the rock we all stood on for support. He didn’t go to college but he was well read and could hold a conversation with anyone, on almost any topic.”

“My oldest sister took mom to make arrangements at the funeral parlor. She picked out a nice wooden coffin with a raised cross on it that was painted gold. That was the best coffin we could afford. The brass ones were very beautiful but really out of our budget. The funeral director had contacted our preacher and he performed the funeral service.”

“After the funeral Mom continued to work at a small local store in the neighborhood. She helped out there part time and it brought in a few extra dollars. Dad’s death benefits helped us a lot since he died while working. But after a while Mom decided that she had to go to work full time; because when she was home alone all she did was think of my father and how much she missed him. So Mom applied to the local post office for a position. They knew my dad and what had happened to him. The postmaster pulled a few strings and she was given a job as a mail handler. It was hard work for her as she was not a large woman, but she did it.”

“I was the third daughter, after my two older sisters. My younger sister Josiah was still in high school when Dad died and she was coping pretty well with his death. I had just graduated from high school and was looking for a job. My oldest sister Lelu joined the Army so she could travel and they would pay for her college when she got out. While she was in the Army she met her white husband in Germany on a military base and they now have two sons and live in Texas. He is a career soldier and loves it."

"My second oldest sister, Chastity, is a stunning girl, a real beauty. I really think she could have been a model, that's how beautiful I think she is. She got a job as a receptionist for a dentist in midtown, just off Park Avenue. He was a white guy and treated her very nicely. He took a liking to her and they started to date. Eventually they got married and she now lives in Scarsdale with her husband, their one daughter, and her Mercedes Benz. Once a month she calls home to speak to my mother; and I am very disappointed in her. She married rich and forgot where she came from."

"We were a very middle class working family trying to make it in New York. We weren't involved in drugs or gangs and didn't live in the projects. My folks rented an apartment over a store in a very nice six family building in Harlem, and we were no different than many other people who lived in the area. Our apartment was nicely furnished with sale items from the cheaper department stores but it still was pretty nice looking."

"After my Dad died I had just graduated from high school and I applied for a front desk job in a new hotel they just built in Manhattan; half a block off of Times Square. I really had no experience but the hotel human resources person offered me a position doing house cleaning instead. I quickly took it with the intention of working my way up the ladder. I am a hard worker and I am very ambitious."

"I started cleaning the guest rooms. I was good at changing the sheets, cleaning the bathrooms and stocking the personal health items by the sinks. It wasn't hard work, just boring. But if someone was a slob it just made it more difficult for me, especially if they were drunk the night before and threw up all over the carpet. That was disgusting to clean up, and it stunk too. I didn't take shortcuts like some of the other girls did. If the sheets did not look dirty they would just pull them tight, fluff the pillows and throw the comforter back on it and leave."

"Every room I cleaned I always pulled the bed apart and changed everything. It was a lot of extra work but I didn't want to get caught cheating. I heard that sometimes the management marked the sheets and would come in to spot check it on the girls. It wasn't worth losing the job."

"As you can see I am not a large woman. I am built like my mother. I'm five foot seven and one hundred and twenty five pounds. Pulling apart thirty or forty beds a day and cleaning a room in twenty minutes or less is not easy. And then you have to do it again the next day. It can be very boring and tiring. I had to hustle to keep the job and make an impression on the supervisor."

"After my first year there I asked the HR lady to see if there was somewhere else I could work in the hotel. I had good write-ups and I told her I wanted to learn all there was about the hotel. I very much wanted to advance my career. So to round out my learning she transferred me to the kitchen to start as a helper. I was instructed on how to cut and clean vegetables, prepare meats for cooking, and everything else that goes on in a kitchen. I was in their kitchen for six days every week. By the time I left the kitchen, after a few years, I was cooking and preparing the food under the supervision of Raoul, who was the executive head chef."

"He was from New Orleans and his special dishes always had a southern flair and flavor to them. They were spicy and fresh and a delight to eat. I know he took a liking to me because I almost married him."

"When the evening shift was over he would prepare a meal for us and we ate it in the small employee dining room next to the kitchen. He always made something special for me for dinner and he was very attentive in helping me learn the different crafts in the kitchen."

"After a while, when we finished eating and it was past midnight, I would ask Veneshia at the front desk if she had any empty rooms she could reserve for us. She would put a dirty tag on it in the computer so no one else would put someone in it. After midnight most of the cleaning girls had all left for the day and only one or two were still on duty for overnight. Only one maintenance man was available and he didn't clean rooms."

"Anyway after midnight there were only a few rooms that would be available to be rented out if they weren't already. They were usually reserved for late flights in from Kennedy or one of the other airports."

"I still had my room cleaning passkey and I made sure to update it once a month after they changed the codes. So Raoul and I would go up to the room and be alone together. Every now and then Raoul made something really outrageous for Veneshia to eat. He would call her to have it on her dinner break in the staff kitchen. She would then get us the penthouse to play in if it was not rented out. But that did not happen too often."

"Raoul and I even started to talk about marriage, but we never set a date or anything. Just we talked about it."

"My life fell into a daily routine of cooking and evening sex until I got a promotion to be an assistant manager in training. They moved me around a lot in the hotel doing all kinds of back office and front desk work. I was lucky because they usually only did that for people with a college degree in hospitality. But they knew me after all those years and I got the position."

"I showed up for work every day on time, did whatever shifts they asked me to work, and I was learning a lot. Then on a quiet Tuesday afternoon I received a phone call from the police."

"They said my older sister Lelu and Mom were in a car accident and were in the hospital. My Mom always drove because my older sister did not have a driver's license. She was visiting us from Texas so I left work immediately and took the subway uptown to the emergency room where they were brought."

"What I didn't know was that she left the Army, her husband and her kids. She took up drinking and was working as a cheap escort to pay the bills and get her booze. But I didn't find that out till much later."

"When I got there my sister Josiah was sitting in the waiting area. She said a stolen car was being chased by the police and it went through a red light and hit their car in the middle, by the driver's side door. The fire department had to cut them out of the car to put them in the ambulance."

"The sounds of the hospital faded into the background as I sat in silence waiting for the doctor to come out and tell us how they were. I heard no noise; it was a very strange feeling."

Shaniqua sat there for a moment in silence, thinking about that afternoon.

The other people in the circle just listened without questioning her. They waited in anticipation for her to continue.

“Finally” she spoke, “the doctor came out to see us.”

“He said that the stolen car must have been speeding very fast as the car was hit in the middle and pushed into oncoming traffic that then slammed into my sister’s side of the car.”

“Both of them”, he said, “suffered severe internal injuries. He couldn’t save my mother but he felt he would be able to save my sister Lelu. She was in surgery and he felt she would make it.”

“She did survive but had to have a steel rod put in her leg and pins in her forearm as she broke her wrist in ten places.”

“It took months for her to get better and then months of physical therapy for her. Almost a year past before she was able to say she felt somewhat better. She is in constant pain and she now walks with a limp; and she also has severe nerve damage in her hand and wrist. If you touch the top of her hand she has a tingling sensation and pulls it away.”

“Our family was devastated after this accident. And my Mom’s funeral was unbearable. Lelu was still in the hospital when we buried mom. She was not able to attend.”

“My sister Lelu started to rely on pain pills for so long that she became addicted to them. She couldn’t function with them, and couldn’t live without them. We were afraid she would overdose someday. He husband had previously left her and took the kids because he felt she had become an alcoholic.”

“Lelu moved in with me and got a job in the neighborhood in a drug store working behind the counter.”

“Then Lelu started to drink again when she got home from work. Luckily she only worked in a store around the corner from us. She couldn’t walk any great distance now with her leg injury. Mom was gone and there was no one home anymore to cook for us. We all grew up very quickly. My sister Lelu now started to drink to numb the loneliness and pain. That mixture of pain pills and alcohol was a bad combination. She started to do some crazy things when she was alone. I once came home and a strange man was ringing my bell. He had answered an online ad and was coming to see Lelu for what he said was 'a fun time'. I couldn't believe she was bringing strange men into our home. You better believe there was a big blowup that night when I walked in and she was in a see through nightgown."

"And if that was not enough on my mind, at work Raoul found a new young waitress to fool around with. She had just turned nineteen and was doing him at least twice a day. He stopped seeing me and I felt very sad and angry toward shim."

"I was working crazy hours, sometimes around the clock, and I was exhausted. The money was good but as part of management there was no overtime, just recognition."

"One day at the hotel this guest was registering and he saw me at the end of the front desk looking at the computer, and he came over to me. He was cute as hell and the first thing he said to me was that he liked to dance and would I like to go dancing tonight with him that night after work? I glanced up at him and it was instant love at first sight for me."

"I never dated a white guy before but he was really good looking, cute, spoke well and most importantly, he smelled great! So I smiled when he said that to me and when he asked me out for dinner that night I said yes. I just had a feeling about him that I never had before."

Jose chirped in and asked where they went. He said he knew most of the in hot spots because he ate at most of them when he was with Johnson.

Shaniqua answered "he waited until I got off that night and we went to the hotel restaurant on the top floor overlooking Times Square. We ordered some cocktails and we talked. As a church girl I never had alcohol before, but since I had already sinned with Raoul, I figured I might as well continue sinning. He was single, never married, and he told me he had just broken off with his girlfriend of two years. He said he had caught her cheating on him so he walked away from their relationship. I think that was the start of our bonding together."

"After dinner we went to a club in midtown and we danced for a while. It was already in the early morning hours and I was having a lot of fun. I really had a great time and when we sat down to relax for a moment in a darkened booth at the back of the club he leaned over and gently kissed me. I was happy that he did that. I really dug him. When we were finished dancing at the club we hopped into a cab and went back to his hotel room for the rest of the night."

"His room was on the top presidential floor; and it was one of our better luxury suites with a fully stocked bar and an oversized tub for two. We both decided to get in the tub together and we kissed again."

"It was the first time I ever had sex with a white guy, and I really enjoyed it. His body was muscular and as he held me close to him I couldn't stop kissing him. I felt his arousal and that just turned me on more. We did not get much sleep that night."

"In the morning we woke up about eleven and we had breakfast together in the coffee shop. He leaned over to me and kissed me again. He smiled at me and whispered in my ear that he 'loves brown sugar'. I kissed him on his lips and slid my tongue into his mouth, just because I wanted to. After that night I saw him every night while he stayed at the hotel. I couldn't get enough of him."

"His name was Eric Raeburn and he was the nicest guy I had ever met. He treated me like a lady, paid for our dinners, and he even opened doors for me when we went somewhere."

"He came to town often after that night. We sometimes went to see Broadway shows, Lincoln Center, or just hung out at my apartment when we wanted to have quiet times alone. Often on my day off we walked in Central Park or visited a museum. I brought a bag lunch some times and we usually sat on a bench under a shade tree and we ate like two love struck teenagers. I really enjoyed those times we had."

"Eric lived in Maryland and worked for a defense contractor in Washington D.C. who sent him to New York and the West Coast on business trips very often. I saw him at least once a month when he was here on business and sometime twice a month. On alternate weeks either I drove down to see him on my days off during the week or he drove up here on weekends. We did that for six months until I got tired of all that commuting so I asked him if he wanted to make a commitment to me. I said I would move to Maryland and get a job there just so I could be with him. He said yes to the commitment suggestion."

"When he was in town the next time he took a cab to the diamond district in midtown Manhattan and bought me a diamond engagement ring. I was thrilled and I wore that ring all the time and I never took it off. I wear it even now, see" as she held out her left hand with the ring on it.

His family is Episcopalian and I am a Baptist, but it didn't matter to us."

"He gave me the ring the same day that he bought it and I was so happy. I took the bus uptown to show my sister Lelu. But when I got off the bus and turned the corner to my block I saw an ambulance taking her out of the house. Police were there too."

"I ran over and told the officer in charge I was her sister. The first thing he said to me was he was sorry about the loss of my sister. He said that there was a push in robbery and she must have resisted. I thought that maybe it one of the men Lelu was contacting online and it went too far. I didn't know for sure, but I told the detective my thoughts anyway. I never heard from him about it since that day. The police officer who was in charge said there was a large gash on the side of her head where she was hit with something hard. He said he thought she fell and was probably dead before she hit the floor."

"The blood drained from my body and I felt faint when he said that to me. I held on to the iron railing by my stoop and slowly sat down on the concrete steps. I was in total shock. I couldn't believe it."

"After the police finished inside my home I went in and sat down, tears rolling down my face. My most happy day turned into a day of grief and sorrow. I called my sister Chastity and she came over immediately. Eric was already on the New Jersey Turnpike back to Maryland when I called him that night to tell him. He offered to turn around but I told him not to. Although I loved him, I just wanted to be with my sister at that moment."

Jose asked if they ever caught the guy that broke into her family's house.

"No" she answered. "The cops said there was a rash of them in that neighborhood and the chances of catching him were slim, unless there was a surveillance camera nearby, and there wasn't. But I knew better. I knew it had to be one of the men that had contacted her for sex."

"When I went in the house it was a wreck. All the drawers in the house were open and clothes were thrown all over. It was a total mess. But what really bothered me were the blood stains on the living room carpet where she had fallen and died. When I saw that I couldn't stop crying. I was devastated."

"I found out a few days later that a neighbor on the top floor was walking downstairs when she saw our front door was open. She was the one who called the police."

"My sister Chastity came over right away when I called her and we went together to see our pastor. After that meeting we then made arrangements at the funeral home near the house, right off of Broadway on a side street. It was the same one that buried my parents."

"Eric came up for the funeral and he sat next to me when our family and friends came to pay their respects. Some of them looked at us strangely since we were the only interracial couple in the place. But no one said anything and he held my hand all the time. I loved him even more, if that was at all possible."

"A few weeks after the funeral when things quieted down Eric and I went for lunch in Greenwich Village at an intimate bistro and we decided on a wedding date. It was a small café and we sat near the window. I ordered the soup of the day and he had an organic roast beef sandwich on rye bread with spicy mustard. He usually ordered that if it was available. Then as we started to talk the real hard part popped up, as to where we were going to get married, and who to invite. In all the months that we were dating I had never met his family. So we decided to drive down together the next weekend and I was going to meet them."

"The ride was uneventful. The New Jersey Turnpike has to be one of the most boring highways in the country. There was nothing much to look at except for the slew of crazy drivers speeding and weaving between cars and trucks at high speed."

"Finally we went over a bridge and we were in Delaware. He got off the highway and took some back roads until I saw a sign that said we were in Maryland. I really wasn't paying much attention because I fell asleep a few times in the car from boredom."

"When we pulled up in front of his parent's house I looked at their home. It was like right out of a picture book. I saw the over grown trees in the front yard with their branches spread out and the green leaves shading the house. The road in front was very narrow, like a quant old time village road, with no sidewalks. They even had a small white wooden fence in the front yard."

"Before I got out of Eric's car I picked up the large box of Godiva Chocolates that I had bought for them. I spent almost one hundred dollars on it and it was in a beautiful box too. Eric leaned over and kissed me. It was a lingering kiss, tender yet full of passion. He smiled at me as he got out of the car and opened my door for me to get out. He held my hand as we walked up to the front door. He knocked and then we went in."

"Their home was not that big but the furniture was. I guess you could call it colonial, because I never saw anything like that before. At least that's what Eric said it was. Blue and green plaids with high wing back sofas and overstuffed chairs were in the living room. In the family room were a lot of wood tables and family pictures hanging on the walls."

"Eric's father Carl was an office manager for some manufacturing company in the area and he also was a deacon in his church. Both of his parents were very nice and accepting of me. Ginger, his mother, made an early dinner for us as I had to get back to the city to work the early shift the next day. It was truly a home cooked meal and it tasted great."

"After dinner his father said he would be honored to officiate at our wedding. I was very excited when he said that so we did not hesitate and we accepted his offer. On the drive back we decided to finally set a date."

"It was now August and we didn't want to wait too long so we decided on October. I told him I could get a deal with my hotel for the ceremony and reception and he agreed."

"The next day when I was at work I spoke to the events manager during my lunch break and she saved me a lot of money on a package for the wedding. We were not going to have a big affair so we were able to book a smaller event room that was available. I had Eric arrange to come to the hotel on his next business trip in and I made an appointment for us to go over the menu with the catering manager."

The first weekend in September he was driving in to see me. There was an accident on the highway in Delaware and his car was rear ended by a tractor trailer. The impact pushed Eric's car into the back of the truck ahead of him, sandwiching it between the two trucks. Eric was killed instantly."

"When his father Carl called me on my cell phone to tell me of his death, I froze and couldn't believe what he said. This wasn't happening, I said to myself. I was at work at the front desk, and I had to sit down. Tears were welling up and I couldn't stand at the front desk like that for the hotel guests to see me in that condition. I just could not comprehend his death. I was in a complete mental daze."

"It took me a while that day but I eventually stood up and told HR why I had to go home. When I got to my apartment I undressed and fell asleep on my sofa. I had to have slept for hours just from mental exhaustion and stress."

"In just a short time I had lost my mother, my father, my sister had been in a terrible car accident and later killed in a home invasion. And now I lost the love of my life."

"When I woke up the next day I felt nauseous and dry heaved for a few minutes. In the next few days my breasts started to hurt me and I continued to throw up a few times during the day. I didn't know what it was so I went to the clinic near my home."

"They told me I was pregnant. I couldn't believe it. I didn't want to raise a child by myself without Eric, and I became very depressed. I stopped eating and didn't get out of bed unless I had to go to work, and I only went to work grudgingly. That's when my kid sister Chastity came to visit me and see how I was doing. She said I have to pull myself together. I didn't want to eat or work, or even get dressed. She sat on my bed next to me and we talked about things. She was trying to have me get back to my life."

"She called a psychologist and I went to see her with Chastity. Luckily my insurance covered the visit. I was diagnosed as clinically depressed but not suicidal."

"Chastity had read about Doctor Willentz in a newspaper article and she called the institute for me. That is how I got here. And yes, I am three months pregnant."

"Thank you Shaniqua" Doctor Willentz said. "We can understand why you are depressed. I think I can help you with that problem."

"How do you feel about being pregnant with Eric's child?" Doctor Willentz asked her.

"I am sad that I lost Eric but at the same time I will always have him with me in our baby" she answered.

"Does that give you some comfort?" he asked her.

"Yes, it does, but I still miss him."

"You now have to focus on the baby, on life, as it is also your parents living in that child. They are all with you, and always will be" Doctor Willentz told her.

Shaniqua stopped to think about that statement and it seemed to make sense to her. She had never thought about it in that way. She had been so overcome with her tragedies that she found it hard to focus on deeper meanings in life. Slowly she sat back in her chair, closed her eyes and didn't say anything. After a while she sat upright and then smiled to herself.

Nobody said anything as they could feel her pain. There is comfort in knowing that other people could feel for you and understand your emotions.

As Doctor Willentz stood up he asked everyone to please follow him downstairs for dinner.

Some of them took the stairs while some waited for the elevator.

Dinner was a strip steak covered in sautéed onions and candied carrots and peas. There also was a Cornish hen for those who did not want red meat.

After dinner they were allowed to roam the grounds and walk around. The evening country air was refreshing and some of them sat outside on wooden benches looking at the scenery.

Mei and Dawn went back upstairs to relax and went into Dawns room and closed the door. They embraced as they kissed, and both of them had mutually satisfying sex on Dawns bed. They finished before the others came back upstairs for the night.

Chapter Six – Day Three - Amanda

It was early the next morning and after the breakfast cart was brought in they all took what they wanted to eat and sat down at a table. This morning they were having farm fresh scrambled eggs with hash browns, whole wheat toast and bacon. Of course there were also cold cereals if anyone wanted it.

Amanda was a very good looking woman with brown wavy shoulder length hair and a very shapely, firm body. She works out in a gym almost daily and has her long nails and hair done on a weekly basis.

When they were all finished eating Doctor Willentz called them back to the circle and he asked Amanda to please tell them something about herself.

"I grew up in a very dysfunctional home in Pennsylvania. My mother was from Columbia and is a massage therapist, but I think she does more than just rub men's bodies. Her shop was in town, over an insurance office, where cars were always coming and going. My mom is a short heavy set woman and has a huge chest and is always wearing very tight, low cut clothing. Plus we were never allowed to visit her at work when she had business hours. She had a big sign in her office that she only took cash, never credit cards or checks. The reason, I think, was that she was hooking."

When she said that about her mother being a prostitute the group looked at her in amazement. Her honesty just shocked everyone.

"Once I was dating" Amanda continued, "and sleeping with a local cop, who was married, and he told me my mom was under investigation for prostitution. But I didn't tell her anything about it. My relationship with her was never great so I decided to let the chips fall where they may. I was almost out of the house already and it would have no effect on me."

"My father was a parochial school teacher. He always had odd jobs after school was over, in the afternoons and evenings. Sometimes when he came home during the summer, when school was out, he was always very tanned from going to the beach. But he never had a tan line anywhere. When I got older he told me he went to a private nude beach in the next town over and that was why he didn't have tan lines. But one afternoon when I was in high school he got a phone call and I heard it was a woman's voice. He walked outside to take the call. So I am almost positive he was having an affair behind my mother's back. I wouldn't be surprised if he walked around naked with his girlfriend at her house."

"Anyway, in school I was in the slower classes as I was not the greatest student. I just got by and graduated with a general diploma. In high school I dated a lot of boys and I slept with almost every one of them; including Mr. Dunn who was my homeroom and science teacher in my junior year of high school."

"He used to flirt with me every morning and he was kinda cute too. He had thinning gray hair but a great body. He once told the class he worked out every day at the gym after school let out. I always flirted back with him, it was a fun thing to do, I thought."

"One afternoon after classes were finished I forgot something in my locker, which was right outside his classroom door. He was standing by the door ready to lock it when he saw me. Jokingly he asked me if I wanted an A in his science class. I smiled and said yes. I knew where this was leading so I walked up to him and got real close. We were almost nose to nose when I placed my hand over his pants zipper and gently stroked him, and he got amazingly hard."

"We went into his classroom where I slowly unbuttoned my blouse and took it off. I turned around to face him and he then started to fondle and kiss my breasts, licking them all around. I slipped off my panties as I hopped on his desk and began to lie back while spreading my legs apart in the air. He leaned over and put his head between my legs and started to lick me there. His tongue swirled around me and I started to climax. He dropped his pants and started to thrust quickly and violently. The final dismissal bell rang just as he was coming inside me. He kept his word and I aced that class. Of course we met weekly until the semester was over. He usually took more time when we met and he was a good lover. He always liked to perform oral sex on me."

"When I was a senior in high school I was always late for school. So the dean of girls sent me to see the principal about it. The dean was fed up with me and didn't know what to do about it anymore. I was warned by her that I could be sent to detention for a long time and it would go on my permanent record. I really couldn't care less about it, but I went to see the principal anyway."

"I remember when I entered the general office to see that old fart. Dr. Abbotto's office was behind the outer office; and I was wearing my really short green skirt that drove the football team nuts whenever I walked by their practice. And the matching tee shirt was form fitting around my D cup bra."

"I had to wait a few minutes in the general office until he was ready to see me. The old pink haired lady that was his secretary told me I could go in now so I stood up, inhaled to expand my chest, and opened his door. As I walked in he closed the heavy solid wood door behind me, turned me around and started to kiss me. I really didn't expect that. He was nice looking for an older man, like my grandfather, but I kissed him back. We exchanged saliva and tongued each other for a while as I rubbed his pants. He locked his office door and took me to his leather sofa by the side wall in the office. He must have been in his early sixties, but he was still pretty good looking, though."

"Dr. Abbotto slipped my tee shirt over my head, flipped my tits out of the bra and started to suck on them as he fingered me. I usually do not wear panties, just a G string, and I started to get really wet. He unzipped his pants and I blew him in his office. Then he got a phone call and he stood up, told me not to be late again, and I got dressed and left."

"As I said I was not a great student and my father once got a letter home from my school guidance counselor that I was failing two subjects and might not graduate if I didn't pass them. He told me that I had to really try harder and he didn't want me to spend another year in high school that wasn't needed."

"I knew I could never pass those classes, even though I was not in the academic program, but would get a general diploma. So I decided to make an appointment with the school principal, Dr. Abbotto, to discuss my situation."

"He saw me in the hallway before my appointment and said I was to meet him in the mall parking lot after school, by the main entrance. He would pick me up there."

"I was driving my boyfriend's car and I drove over to the mall and waited for him. He spotted me and drove over and opened his passenger door for me to get in. We drove to some cheap motel nearby and he parked in the back where nobody could drive by and accidently see his car. He already had a room key and we went into the motel room together."

"He undressed, and I did too. He put his arms around me and embraced me. We kissed a little until he had me get on my knees, and I blew him again, swallowing all of it. When he was finished he picked me up and placed me on the bed. He started to kiss my feet, suck my toes, and even between my toes. To be honest it did nothing for me but it excited him. His tongue darted in and out, licking them all over. I never had that happen to me before, and it felt odd, yet it was kind of arousing. He continued to suck on my toes and at one point he put all my toes in his mouth and swished his tongue around them. He did that for almost twenty minutes. I saw him start to get aroused and he moved his face up and started to lick my inner thighs and my outer lips. When I started to move my body and get excited he slid his body up and entered me. He was much larger than any of the boys on the football team, and he really knew how to turn me on."

"We spent almost two hours in that motel room having sex. When we were getting dressed I mentioned to him that I was failing two classes and needed to pass them in order to graduate. He smiled and said not to worry about it; he would take care of it. And he right then made another appointment with me for the next week, which I realized I had to keep. This went on weekly for two and a half months until graduation. Then I didn't see him during the summer, unless I was feeling horny and called him at summer school; which I did every now and then. He was married so he never called me."

Dawn just listened in amazement. She had never imagined that a school principal would sleep with a student, and blackmail her for sex. Growing up in a somewhat strict home she was always the nerdy mousey kid in school who never even thought about sex until she met Marcus.

"Did you ever sleep with a girl?" asked Dawn.

"Only once" she answered. "I had applied for my first job in Manhattan as a receptionist for a Madison Avenue advertising company. They were way up on one of the top floors of an office building with floor to ceiling glass walls and windows. If you stood there looking down, out onto midtown Manhattan, you felt as if there was no window and you could just fly away. What a great view from the lobby of that office."

"I had called them about an ad I saw online and I had an eleven o'clock appointment with their human resources lady. When I arrived I was taken into a small office and given a pre-employment form to fill out."

"When I was finished filling it out I walked over and handed it to an older girl at the front desk. She told me to wait a few minutes and Miss Vasquez would be right with me."

"After a few minutes she came out of her office and introduced herself. She was about five foot five with close cropped hair, no tits to speak of, and an almost boyish hair style with a tight fitting pants suit on. She had a tight artificial smile, shook my hand, and brought me into her office; and we both sat down to talk."

"She noticed on my application that I had no experience but she said I could be trained. It was not too big a factor, she said as she looked at me kind of funny. I didn't realize then that she had a double meaning to what she had said to me."

"Then Miss Vasquez asked where I was living and I told her I was living at the YWCA with a roommate. I had no other place to live as I really wanted to leave home and not look back."

"Miss Vasquez told me what the job paid and I thought it was a lot of money for someone with no experience. She said I might be able to get the position, if I played my cards right. I was not sure what she meant, but I soon found out."

"She coyly smiled and asked me if I would like to get a drink with her after work, and she would pay. It would be in about thirty minutes so I said okay. Why not, I thought, she was paying and I had nowhere else to go."

"The door to their lobby was right behind me so I walked into the waiting room very happy to get a position."

"I sat in the outer waiting room for her to finish her day. But I did notice that her secretary looked at me strangely when I left her office. It was like she was throwing daggers at me with her eyes. But I didn't pay any attention to her. Just another old jealous bitch with no tits, fuck her, I thought to myself."

"When Miss Vasquez was finally finished she came out to apologize for being a little late and we both walked to the elevator together. I noticed her secretary was not smiling as we left her office."

"We walked out of the building together at five thirty in the afternoon. As we stood on the sidewalk she hailed a cab and she took me to a very noisy small midtown bar filled with women; and the music was way too loud. But yet it didn't seem too weird to me, other than there were no men in the bar and it was filling up quickly with girls."

"Miss Vasquez said I could call her Juanita or Juan if I wanted to shorten it. It was then that I realized she was butch, but I was already here with her and she bought the drinks for both of us. So I just relaxed a bit and enjoyed the liquor."

Mei was curious and asked if Amanda had slept with Miss Vasquez?

"Well" Amanda answered, "Yes I did. It was that night, but much later in the evening. I was feeling a little tipsy and I probably drank a little too much. So she walked with me out of the bar holding my arm tightly. She suggested that I go with her up to her apartment that was around the corner until I could sober up."

"As I approached the apartment house the doorman opened the door for us and said good evening. I was impressed. When we got off the elevator and entered her apartment I walked into her living room and I sat down on the sofa. It was a very masculine room with brown leather chairs and dark touches everywhere. The sofa was in real cowhide and there were bronze statues of cowboys on horses all around the room. It was not feminine in any way."

"I was really feeling tired and the drinks were taking their toll on my judgment. I leaned my head back on her sofa and started to close my eyes. Juanita sat down next to me and started to kiss my neck, and then when I didn't stop her, she kissed me on the lips."

"Maybe I was drunk, but it felt good, so I didn't stop her. Her hands were amazing and the warmth of her tongue in my mouth felt good. It was very exciting kissing her as she found my honey spot and sent me into orgasm after orgasm."

"The next thing I remember was the following morning after she had left for work and I was alone in her bed…totally naked. That night was a total blank except I do remember some flashbacks of having an orgasm or two. But I really don't remember much else. My clothes were neatly draped over a bedroom chair next to her dresser."

"Her phone rang and the answering machine came on and it was her asking me to pick up the phone. I did and she said she had a good time last night and if I wanted to stay over till she came home we could go out to a great steak place she knows of for dinner."

"I was tired, a little sore down there, and said to myself 'what the hell might as well stay' so I agreed to wait for her in her apartment."

"So you became a lesbian after that night?" Mei asked.

"Yer, I guess you could say that. But she was the only woman I ever slept with. I stayed there for a few days and we had a good time together that week. We went out as a couple to restaurants and she even bought tickets for us to a Broadway play. I had a great time with her. I was her new plaything."

"The job at her company never happened. She didn't get me the position with her firm because she said we were too sexually involved and she thought it would be a distraction to her. I was hoping that I could use my week with her to get that high paying job she had interviewed me for. But she couldn't, and I understand it."

"She did make a phone call for me and did get me a job interview with a friend of hers at another midtown company, as a manager in training. The pay was the same that she had offered me and there were men running the company. That phone call started my next job adventure in New York. What happened to me next I never expected."

"I had put down that I was a college graduate from Rutgers in New Brunswick and I got a position as a manager in training for their company. Their HR person didn't know Juanita but the COO did. Mr. Bruce Donnelly the COO was her ex-husband and he hired me as a favor to her. I have a feeling that now and then they get together, but I don't know for sure."

"So the human resource manager at Mr. Donnelly's firm tried to verify my college records and when he couldn't the HR manager called me in to his office; and he asked me about where I went to college. I am not totally stupid. I was smart enough to get a curriculum guide to the school of business at Rutgers. I remembered some course names and professors that taught them. I gave him that information and said I can't help it if they can't find me in their system. They are a huge university and students run the back office there. So eventually he gave up and stopped asking me questions about my qualifications."

"Anyway Mr. Bruce Donnelly, the COO, also interviewed me and he took a liking to me. And he was the one who actually hired me. After the interview he asked me to have lunch with him on his lunch break. He was much older than Juanita but that was okay. I have a thing for older men anyway. As his ex-wife Juanita was a butch lesbian, he knew I had to be a lesbian also. But I really liked guys. Although I had fun with Juanita I don't consider myself a true lesbian."

"He escorted me down to the lobby and took me in his private chauffeured limousine to a famous steak house in midtown Manhattan. We were seated together in a dark booth in the back of the restaurant, off to the side. The booth, although it was curved, was on the small side and we sat very close to one another. So close that our thighs actually touched each other. Based on the small talk we had I sensed that he was horny and would try to make a play for me. There were a few double meanings on some of his sentences and I picked up on them."

"He was asking me questions about Juanita and stuff and I had to truthfully answer that I had only just met her about a week or so ago. He said that he might have expected that as her steady girlfriend was away on business in California; so that is why she found a new toy to play with. But she had to hide me since her girlfriend was coming back. That was why she had called him to hire me."

"He asked me if I ever dated men, and I knew what he wanted, so I answered him by placing my hand on his lap, and then slowly I moved it over to his inner thigh."

"He reminded me of Dr. Abbotto back in high school. Bruce was a mature executive with wavy gray hair brushed back and wore an expensive two thousand dollar business suit. On his left wrist he wore a gold Rolex watch with diamonds going around the watch face. It was a beautiful watch; it must have been very expensive."

"Then Bruce carefully took my hand and placed it on his crotch, and I started to squeeze it very slowly and gently until I felt his manhood stiffen. To tease him and get him nuts I would stop stroking him and lift my hand up when I thought he was getting too aroused. I think this drove him crazy. He started to squirm in the booth and he placed his hand on my lap and then went under my dress with it. He found my honey spot and started to rub it until I got very excited. I was straining not to moan out loud. Finally I had to move his hand away as I was about to lose it and moan loudly in the restaurant, I couldn't restrain myself any longer. He was doing to me what I had just done to him."

"Finally he got the idea and asked for the check. It came just in time as I was about to squirt and wet myself in the booth. We hurriedly left the restaurant and instead of going back to work he called in to his secretary that he will be out on business; and we went to his apartment on Park Avenue to fool around."

"Park Avenue in Manhattan is a very expensive place to live. They not only had a doorman to open the outer doors, but one to open the inner doors also. They had a concierge desk that took in and held the mail and packages for the people who lived there. They also screened everyone that entered and would call up before they let anyone enter thc hallway by the elevators."

"As soon as we went into his apartment he started to undress, and so did I. He pulled me close to him in an obsessive embrace and he started to fondle me; and with his left hand he softly rubbed my honey spot again until I started to squirm. He then took me by my hand and we walked into his bedroom. It was a very masculine looking room with rich wood furniture and a four poster bed in the middle. He placed me on the side of the bed and had me sit up on it. Bruce then kneeled down and spread my legs so his face could get in there."

"We had sex for the next hour or so and he was moaning and clinching his teeth every time we did it. I made sure he came at least three times. I knew he had money and I wanted to be his baby doll. Hell, why work if you could just have sex and live like that!"

"I know exactly what you are saying" Mei chirped in.

"I slept tin is bed with him that night and he called a cab for me early in the morning so I could go to work before he did. When he finally arrived at work he called me into his office. I closed the door behind me and he put his arms around me and we kissed, and fondled each other. I knelt down, unzipped his pants, and blew him right there in his office. It was ten in the morning and he had a woody. I stood up afterwards and asked if he would like me to move in with him? Hell… I already knew the answer from the smile on his face."

"I really couldn't do the job that was required of me but they couldn't fire me as I was not only sleeping with the boss but living with him. And if they did, I think it could be considered sexual harassment on their part, but I'm not sure. And I do know that the upper managers desperately wanted to get rid of me, but they didn't know how without jeopardizing their positions in the company. I was really screwing up my work as I didn't know what I was doing."

"Finally they thought up a way to dump me and not piss off the boss. They came up with a severance package because they said they had to cut back. I didn't want to ask my lover if it was true because I knew sooner or later he would dump me for another pretty face."

"I got one year's salary and paid benefits for one year to leave their company. I took it and moved out of his apartment the next day and back into the Y. Not bad for only four weeks work."

"Living with Bruce was okay at first but he really couldn't get it up on a consistent basis. The first few days were great but then he went limp. I felt that I needed more sexually, and with the money the managers arranged for me to get I was okay leaving him."

"Looking back at it I am not sure if I made a mistake, or not, by leaving him. But I did what I thought was the best thing to do at the time, for me."

"But I still received phone calls from him very often. I had made it a point to stand on the sidewalk by the corner of his building every so often when he was going home from work so that he could see me."

"We dated a few times after that if I wanted a fancy meal and I was also a frequent overnight guest in his apartment when he got really horny."

"And the jewelry he gave me after a date was always appreciated. He had an account at this custom jeweler on Madison Avenue and he took me there a lot. Bruce bought me expensive watches and rings and a few gold bracelets also. And I made sure I thanked him in a way that he really would like. He especially loved it when I thanked him orally."

"He was always begging me to move back in with him but I wasn't desperate. If I was at the end of my rope, I think I would just move back with him and stay there."

"That's about the time when my grandmother got sick and asked me to live in her apartment to watch over it. My dad had her moved into a nursing home for a while and she could not live in her home alone anymore. All her furniture and things were there for me to use. They were real old fashioned stuff, too. She moved out and lived in the nursing home until she was able to move in with my father's brother in Westchester."

"I really didn't want to live in her place but it was a six room apartment over a bar that she used to own. Years ago after my grandfather died my father and his brother talked her into selling the building she owned. Part of the sale stated that there was a clause she could live there, and her heirs could live there, but not rent it out. No one in my family got along with my grandmother. It was my dad's mother and she was a real bitch. Once I moved in she accused me of selling her things and keeping the money. I didn't sell anything of hers, I just threw it out it because it was so old and it smelled like an old lady!"

"I was living there rent free because that was part of the deal. My grandmother could live there for her lifetime plus thirty years rent free. So I really had no expenses except utilities and food."

"Once I met this fellow on line and we set up a date to go to the movies on a Thursday night. As you can see I have a habit of constantly talking. During the movie he got up to go to the bathroom and never came back. I was pissed, but at least he bought me popcorn and I got to see a movie for free. What a schmuck! He could have gotten laid that night, it was his loss."

"I don't know why but I started to follow him the next day. I knew where he lived, and I just followed him when he went to work. I also started hanging around by his house when he came home too, although I never called out to him what a prick he was."

Doctor Willentz interrupted her and told her that what she did was considered stalking.

"I know. I did it before in high school. I had a crush on this boy and we went out a few times, had sex with him, and then he dumped me. He said I was crazy, but I was good enough for him to bang a few times, wasn't I? When I would drive slowly by his house and he was outside he would start to throw rocks at my car. But I didn't stop going to his house. So I continued to follow him until his parents called the police and got a restraining order of protection against me. Then I stopped because I had to."

"I was now living rent free in Manhattan and I had my severance money to keep me going for a while. And Bruce was always there if I needed some extra cash. But I really needed a job because I was bored just hanging out, so I applied for a management position at this travel company and I got it."

"I told them I majored in travel in college, but I really didn't. I never even went to college. I barely graduated from high school. They never checked and I just had to make sure things were going smoothly in the office. The people there were already working and knew what they were doing. Plus I got paid to watch them and fill out a few reports, which I never did."

"When the head office in Florida called to see where my reports were I told them that I asked the staff people to fill out their section of the reports and send it in. I felt they should be responsible for their work, not me. That didn't go over too well, but I never filled them out or sent them in. I had the staff people do it."

"Part of the pay package was free travel and after six months I took a free cruise to the Islands. It was on that cruise that I met Pedro Martinez. He was a young Mexican businessman from Guadalajara that I met at the pool. He was very handsome and dark looking with six pack abs. And he noticed me."

"I was on the top tier swim deck which was a clothes optional pool. I expected someone to notice me, and I was glad it was him. He took off his trunks and jumped in next to me. He was very handsome and he looked at me and started to smile. That was enough to get my attention. I swam over to him and put my arms around his neck as I pressed my chest into his. I started to kiss him and grind my body into pelvis. He placed his hand under the water and started to rub me and I got very excited. Needless to say so did he, because I started to then stroke him under the water also."

"We both decided to get out of the pool and I followed him to his stateroom on an upper deck. He had a balcony and a large suite of paneled rooms with a huge shower. My room was an inner one on a lower deck with no window. For free I guess I couldn't complain."

"I dropped my bathing suit on the floor and hoped onto his bed where he then spread my legs and started to lick my inner thighs, very slowly. As his face moved upwards and finally arrived where I knew he was going, I was already moving and feeling an orgasm coming on. He bent over me as he entered me and we started to kiss. That afternoon I had too many orgasms to even begin to count. And I let him do whatever he wanted, wherever he wanted, and I don't regret a thing.

"We had dinner together that night, did a little dancing in the disco and then we went back to his room for some more intimate playtime. He said he was buying a condo in Manhattan when he got back to New York and he told me the condo address he was looking at, which was a big mistake on his part. I guess what

Doctor Willentz said is true because I started to follow him once we got back to New York."

"I guess I am a stalker. He told me he didn't want to see me anymore when I greeted him at the door to his condo building. He said, with his Mexican accent, that it was just a vacation fling for him and nothing more."

"Those are exactly the words that the judge also said to me when Pedro pressed charges against me; and got a restraining order of protection. I was given a choice of one year in jail, or a treatment program since I had a prior history of stalking. After all this was my second order of protection by someone I was stalking. My lawyer recommended this treatment program, so here I am!"

"Thank you, Amanda" Doctor Willentz said in his firm yet kind masculine voice.

"Amanda, why do you think you stalk these men?" Doctor Willentz asked her.

"I never thought about why I stalk them. I guess I am intrigued, curious, why they didn't want me, I guess is the answer" she said to the doctor.

"Maybe" Doctor Willentz said, "this is your way of wanting the closeness that you never had with your parents. Wanting them to want you, and you are trying to get that reaction from these men that distanced themselves from you. I would like you to think about that."

"Some things in life" he continued, "are just out of your control and you have to deal with it on an adult level. It is what it is and you can't force someone to change their minds and like you" he concluded.

"Okay" Amanda said, contemplating what he told her. But you could see it didn't sink in. Doctor Willentz couldn't put in her head what God didn't.

He continued talking and trying to get through to her. But he soon realized this would take a lot more time than one week of group therapy. Finally he announced "its lunch time and the lunch cart will be here shortly. Why doesn't everyone take a few minutes to gather their thoughts and we'll meet back here in fifteen minutes or so to eat lunch?"

"Either sit by the windows or you can go back to your room to write to family or relax a bit quietly by yourselves and reflect on what was said while you were here this week so far" Doctor Willentz told them.

The floor nurse wasn't there as she had taken her lunch break while Doctor Willentz was with everyone. He sat at a table near the wall and started to write some thoughts he had into his notebook.

Most of the people sat by themselves and either watched the communal television that they turned on or just looked out the window.

Dawn went into her room and closed her door. Mei quietly and quickly followed her in just as the door was closing. Once inside they embraced and started to kiss, darting their tongues back and forth slowly, with desire and lust.

Mei sat down on Dawn's desk chair, spread her legs wide apart, and slipped her robe open exposing herself to Dawn; who quickly knelt down and started to perform oral sex on Mei while also fingering her at the same time. Mei put a rolled up clean wash cloth in her mouth to muffle her groans of ecstasy while Dawn brought her to multiple organism's in very quick succession. Mei was excited and very wet when she started to squirt fluid into Dawns mouth, which Dawn swallowed as she had no other option at the moment. They both understood that it had to be short and quick; and they had to take turns with each other, but not now. The next time they got together it was Dawn's turn to sit back and have Mei satisfy her.

When they were finished Dawn opened her door and the lunch cart was just being wheeled in. Only ten minutes had passed since they closed the door to be together. It was just sex to both of them, raw passion, and with no emotional feelings, they thought. And they both understood what this was.

For lunch today they had a choice of cold turkey sandwiches with potato chips and chicken soup with rice; or a tuna hero with chips and coleslaw on the side.

Mei was kind of tired from her excitement and only took a can of ginger ale and sat by herself next to a window quietly where she rested her head on the back of the chair and closed her eyes..

The rest, including Dawn, took their food and sat together at the lunch tables eating and watching the television. Meanwhile Doctor Willentz continued writing his notes from the morning session. That afternoon he was planning on Barbara telling her life story to everyone.

Chapter Seven – Barbara

After lunch was finished Doctor Willentz called everyone back to the circle to begin their afternoon session.

As usual Barbara was the last to leave the lunch table and sit in her chair in the circle. Today she was even slower because she knew it was her turn.

Reluctantly she waddled over to her chair and sat down; then she pulled her robe as closed as she could. It was not that she is embarrassed to expose herself in public; she had done it many times before, but today seemed different to her. She could not tell her self why, but she knew she had to be emotionally ready to talk about her life. Closing the robe was to her a symbol of bringing in her emotions and her thoughts.

The robe was a three-x size and was almost too small to close, and it just about did close around her. She took in a deep breath and started to talk in a slow, deliberate, manner gathering her thoughts as she spoke.

"I was always a big girl" she started. "When I was born my grandmother told me I was over ten pounds, and very long. And in elementary school I was the tallest and heaviest girl there. I was teased about my weight all through my school years. They used to tell me I was as big as a boy and they called me Bobby, as in a boy's name. I also got into a lot of fights over it. I wouldn't take the taunting and just haul off and slug them, so after a while they steered clear of me."

"My mother worked in a night club as a cook so I really didn't see her much. She would be sleeping when I got up to go to school and she left for work before I got home. My grandmother lived with us and she really raised me. Mom would sometimes come home late on a Sunday morning after being out all night. Then she would kiss me hello when she walked in and go right to bed."

"My mother told me my father was a hero and was killed in a big fire. He was a fireman in the city, the Bronx, I always thought. I never knew him and as I was growing up I idolized him. But there were never any pictures of him, and I did ask my mom about that but I never got a straight answer."

"It was years later, as a teenager, I tried to do some research on him and I couldn't find anything about him. He had no relatives in town and my mother refused to talk about it. When I was fourteen my grandmother finally told me that my mom was raped on a date she had gone on and I was the result of that rape. They never caught the guy, she said he just disappeared, and my grandmother and mother moved from their original home to make sure he didn't come back after her."

"As a fourteen year old girl who her whole life, until then, held an image of her father in her mind only to have it torn apart in five seconds was very upsetting. I was devastated by that information. I felt like my world had collapsed and my image of my father as a hero was ruined."

"And not only that but when I went to our attic to look for my fall sweaters I saw a small box in the corner and opened it. There were nude pictures of my mother and a phone number to call for a date. I realized that my mother was not a cook in a club but a stripper and a prostitute. No wonder she had no idea who my father was. I am the result of a cheap whores date."

"I felt extremely betrayed and I became depressed after reading that. I rebelled and started acting out at school."

"Any boy that wanted some action knew he could count on me. Even the good looking guys came to me when they had an urge… and all I wanted was to feel wanted and have sex with them."

"Luckily I never became pregnant or caught some disgusting sex disease. But I was very loose and in demand during my teenage years. There was nothing I wouldn't do with a boy, just to be with him, or any boy for that matter. Once in high school I was taken into the boy's locker room during gym class by a boy I had screwed before; and I had sex in the shower room with a few of the guys at the same time. I enjoyed that and I never felt funny about it or ashamed. They even gave me money afterwards and after school was out I took the bus and went to Bamberger's in Newark to buy some clothes."

"As I got older I got even taller and bigger. I am now five foot nine and almost four hundred pounds, I think. Because of my stomach I can't see my scale at home, so I really don't know my present weight. But it has to be up there" Barbara continued.

"Anyway when I graduated high school I had no interest in college so I got a job selling mattresses for a large retail mattress chain. It wasn't too bad of a job though. After my initial training was finished I was put into a store by myself. If there were no customers coming in, I could sit down and read the newspaper or a book. It was a very relaxing job for me. Not hard at all."

"I wasn't the size I am now, although I was a large girl, and I did pretty well selling. If it was a slow day I would go to the bakery next door. I'd walk in and buy a double layered chocolate cake with extra icing on top or a dozen iced assorted cupcakes and bring them back for lunch, or to snack on."

"The district manager said I had a knack for selling and I always hit my numbers. He really didn't know how I did all those sales. My manager thought that I was a super salesperson. I even landed in the top twenty salespeople in the company."

"What they did not know was that it helped if a single guy came in. I would offer him an inducement to buy a set of bedding. If he bought the starting numbers I would give him oral sex. For the higher priced luxury mattresses I took him in the back. We had sex on a plastic covered set of bedding. I always wore a dress with a thong underneath it. I never wore panties. So I only had to lift the skirt and slide the thong to the side."

"One month I was the number one selling salesperson in the whole company. And they were almost a national chain with over three hundred and forty stores in twenty odd states. Their furthest store was in Chicago. Then they went as far south as New Orleans. I worked my ass off that month, literally; and you should have seen what I did for a premium set of bedding."

"Let me tell you something about the mattress business. My company always took back a set of bedding within thirty days if the customer didn't like it. But if it was stained they didn't. What they did when they took it back was spray a disinfectant on the mattress and then stuffed it into a new plastic bag, and resold it as new. The spray never killed anything; and I saw sets go out with bed bugs on it; and one set smelled of cigarette smoke. Never buy a mattress from a company that lets you try it out and takes it back. Some of the big department stores are good for that also."

"Then one month they put some older salesman in with me, named Roger, because my sales numbers were so high. They felt the store would have bigger sales numbers if they had two people in it. Of course the opposite happened. I couldn't screw my way to sales because he was there; and the store's total sales numbers dropped."

"It not only affected the company's money but mine also. My income took a sharp drop because he cut into my sales action, as I explained before."

"So I did the only thing I could think of in order to increase my sales. I slept with the guy and told him to sell what he could, and I would sell my way. Roger was happy and so was I. Maybe once or twice a week I had to blow him to keep him quiet. And every now and then if he was really horny we went in the back for intercourse, but that didn't happen too often as he had trouble getting it up."

"We worked together as a team for almost a year. Then he had a heart attack while I was screwing him in the rear storage room on a great set of luxury bedding. It was real firm on my ass. Anyway Roger rolled off of me gasping for air. I quickly called 911 for him. Neither of us told the emergency techs what we were doing. They realized he had had a heart attack and quickly gave him oxygen and rushed him to the hospital. He retired shortly after that. Neither one of us ever told the company why he had a heart attack. He was able to retire when he got out of the hospital on disability."

"The company then sent in two people to replace him. I now had a man and a woman working in my store. Again our store sales dropped and my income did also. So I started to look for another position."

"Did you ever have sex with a woman?" Dawn asked.

"No, not at that time I didn't. I had no interest in it then. But then no woman was ever interested in me sexually. I was always so big and fat" Barbara said

"You had lesbian have lesbian sex in your movies, didn't you Dawn?" Barbara asked.

Dawn didn't answer verbally; she sat there and slyly smiled at her. The message was sent.

Barbara then continued "I found a job in the newspaper selling industrial cleaning products for this wholesale distributor in Northern New Jersey. I applied for it and they called me in for an interview."

"Luckily for me the vice president of sales was a chubby chaser and he started to drool when I walked into his office. He had a picture of his wife on his desk and she was a big girl also, she looked almost like a square with no neck. But I was bigger than her. So he was very coy when he was talking to me; and I could tell by the way he was talking that he was interested in more than just hiring me for sales. So I felt I had nothing to lose and I quietly asked him if there was something I could do to help me get the job? I said I was willing to do anything… if it would help."

"He looked at me for a second and asked if I would like to fool around. He said it that way so it was not an outright sexual offer per se. I stood up and lifted my dress exposing myself to him. He came around from the desk and started to kiss and fondle my breasts. I reached down and unzipped his pants and took it out. He sat back on his desk and I knelt over and blew him right there in his office. He hired me on the spot when I was finished."

The company was a small one and they gave me very little training, and then they sent me out with a few samples and a ton of booklets. I had to go to factories, nursing homes and schools trying to sell their products."

"I had no idea what I was selling but I tried and I read all the booklets they gave me. I soon found out it was a very competitive field and there was no bottom price on a lot of things. Our competition dropped prices on almost everything just to get some business. I started to feel down in the dumps again so I would binge eat on a lot of chocolate cake to try and make myself feel better. I really loved it when they put sliced banana circles between the chocolate layers."

"Then about three weeks later I was talking to this apartment complex custodian about some commercial floor wax I was trying to sell to him; and he said he would be interested in buying it from me. But he sat back in his desk chair and asked me what I could do for him to persuade him to make a purchase. I immediately knew what he was looking for. I told him to stand up and drop his pants. It was just like the bedding business again. After that session with the custodian I knew how to make a sale in this field. I was always dealing with men and I now knew how to close that deal."

"Some of the custodians were really good looking guys. I never could figure out why they found me attractive and wanted to have sex with me. I just figured they were chubby chasers and liked my type of woman.

Or they were extremely horny, especially the Spanish guys. They always liked big girls and I certainly qualified."

"So… I once asked a customer why he would sleep with me and he said it had nothing to do with me. It was just sex and that men took advantage of the situation when it arose. I kind of felt bad when he said that. I enjoyed the sex as it was the only way I could feel wanted, but I knew deep in my heart it was a shallow kind of affection, if at all."

"Knowing this I decided to have a little fun and also try to increase my total sale when I was with these guys. I always carried this very expensive high end commercial vacuum cleaner with me. One day when I went to see this particular custodian I brought it in with me. When we were in his office I suggested he buy it so I could show him how to use it, as I smiled and winked at him. Once he bought it and gave me a check I showed him how the extra thick grip handle was easy to manipulate as I inserted it in myself. I lifted my dress and moved my thin thong to the side as I gently slid it in. By this time I could see he was very excited so I finished playing with myself and also finished him off orally."

"I started to set all kinds of vacuum sales records in the company. These were very expensive commercial and industrial duty vacuums. They sold for well over fifteen hundred dollars each, not counting the extra bags they had to buy also. As a matter of fact the vacuum cleaner manufacturer sent me on a cruise that winter to the Caribbean Islands for ten days because I set a new national sales record for them. If they only knew how I did it."

"It was on that cruise that I met my master."

Shaniqua chirped in and asked "you met your what?"

"My master" Barbara answered in a matter of fact manner.

"I never really knew his real name, but I'll explain that in a little while" she answered.

"I was sitting on one of the upper decks on a lounge chair with my legs straight out in front of me looking out at the harbor as the ship sailed out of Miami. This really great looking, mature, gentleman came over to me and stood right in front of me. His hair was a salt and pepper color and he had very chiseled facial features. The blue blazer he had on contrasted nicely with the half unbuttoned white linen shirt with his chest hair showing. He politely asked if it was alright for him to sit on the lounge chair next to mine. I told him it was empty and I did not mind at all. He sat down, smiled at me, and then he opened a newspaper and started to read."

"We didn't talk or even look at each other for a while. It was so relaxing to sit there and listen to the silence, and have the gentle sea breeze blow on my face and cool me off as the ship slowly sailed on to its first port of call."

What Barbara did not realize was that he could not stop looking at her bright pink fleshy upper thighs when she moved her legs, and her skirt slightly shifted up a little. That massive upper leg was a turn on for him.

"Finally" Barbara said, "he turned to me and apologized for his manners. He introduced himself and said his name was John Jefe, but much later I found out that was a lie, it wasn't his real name. But I'll get to that soon enough. I told him my name was Barbara and we started to talk about the cruise and the ports the ship was going to visit."

"Yes" Barbara said out loud, I did think it was an unusual last name but I didn't give it a second thought after that. I thought maybe it was Greek, I had no idea where it was from."

"We engaged in a little meaningless banter then John asked me to join him for dinner that night in the main dining room, and I said yes. I had no plans for dinner and I thought I would rather eat with a handsome good looking man than by myself."

"I had bought a new sequined midnight blue evening dress before I left for the cruise. When I got back to my cabin I took it out and was going to wear it for that night. I showered and did my hair and makeup and I sprayed my favorite perfume that I brought along. I really felt special that evening. My boobs were almost hanging out of my bra but there was nothing I could do about that. I never could find the right fit; so many times I never even bothered to wear one. When I was dressed I left my state room and walked to the elevator to meet him on the main deck. Then we took the next elevator together to the main dining room."

"As we walked off the elevator next to one another he took my hand and we waked into the dining room together as a couple. No man had ever held my hand in his, ever. This was a first for me and I loved it. I felt that he liked me, or at least he was being a gentleman to me. My self-esteem soared when we approached the maître 'd to get seated."

"When we got to our table he pulled out my chair for me to sit and then he pushed it in under me as I sat down."

"Dinner was great. I had a thick prime rib with mushroom gravy and a twice baked cheddar cheese potato with butter and candied tiny round onions. He had a stuffed capon with field vegetables and he ordered a whole bottle of red wine for me and a bottle of white for himself. Needless to say I got plastered."

"After dinner we both walked outside on one of the decks and we stood there at the railing looking out at the sea while the moon was high in the sky. It was very romantic. He gently turned me around and kissed me softly on my lips. He had placed his hand behind my head and slowly pulled me in towards him as we embraced."

"I have to tell you that was my first real kiss from a man. I must have screwed dozens and dozens of men but no one ever kissed me with real emotional feelings. At that moment something in my heart burst; it was beating so hard, I actually felt it. I felt wanted for being just me."

"I put my arms around his neck and with all the passion I had I kissed him back, this time pulling him into me. I felt his hand gently slide down my side and over, stopping between my thighs. He pressed in with his hand and I started to move. He suggested we go back to his stateroom for the rest of the evening, and I agreed."

"He had a very large room with a queen size bed and a private balcony. I walked out onto the balcony and couldn't believe where I was. A great looking man was standing behind me with his arms around me, kissing the back of my neck as he started to unzip my dress."

"As he was kissing me I felt him push into my back with his body as he held me tightly in his arms. I didn't want to move, I was really feeling, at that moment, he wanted me for me and not just for sex."

"I had never experienced anything like that emotion before. I turned around and started to kiss him on his neck. As I did that he gently placed his hand on my thigh and slid it under my skirt. His hand moved slowly up my inner thigh until he found what he wanted to reach."

"I did not want to stop him. Shit, I screwed strangers in the back of the mattress store and I knew they didn't care a rat's ass for me at all. But I felt this was different. I was falling in love with a total stranger that I had only just met that morning."

"He undid my dress and it dropped to the floor as I stood there completely undressed on his private balcony with the sea below me. We walked into the doorway of his bedroom and he undressed; and we embraced again, passionately kissing and touching."

"I suggested we move into the bedroom and he led me to his bed where he kissed me all over. It was dark inside the cabin and only the light from a full moon was shining in. I couldn't see much, just an outline, but I had no need to see anything. I felt everything. He kissed me where no man had ever kissed me, or wanted to. He was my dream lover who had finally come to life."

"That night was the clincher for me. We did everything a normal couple would do that was in love. There was nothing kinky done that night, but I was soon to find out what he had in mind."

"We were a couple on the ship after that first night and I had some very good times with him on that cruise."

"The rest of the cruise went okay also. We stopped at a few islands and walked around together. On St. Thomas he bought me a gold watch and it was really expensive. I saw the price on it and he paid three thousand dollars for my watch. I didn't know what to say, I was speechless. No man ever bought me anything before, let alone an expensive watch like he gave me."

"That night we slept together again and when the ship set sail and left the dock I was in his arms with my legs rapped around him."

"One of the highlights of my cruise was when we were in Aruba and he took me to a nude beach. We were alone except for a few other couples and we had the greatest time there. He brought a blanket from the ship and the concierge packed a food basket and a bottle of wine for us to take with us that day. We sat under a palm tree and ate a delicious lunch completely naked with the water just a few feet from us. It was very romantic. I loved being there with him" Barbara said.

"When the ship returned to Miami we took a plane together back to New Jersey. We arrived at Newark Airport in the late afternoon and he paid for a taxi to take me home."

"He called me that night and we started to date on a steady basis. We always went out a few times during the week for dinner, or a small club for drinks, and then back to his condo in Edgewater for sex."

"I was still selling for the commercial cleaning distributor and still sleeping my way to sales. There was this large supermarket account they had for paper supplies. They were buying toilet paper and towels from us but the cleaning fluids and hand soaps from someone else. The key words are 'they were' buying their cleaning supplies from someone else."

"I had already sold them their large commercial vacuums and floor scrubbers but now I wanted their liquid business also. That is where the high volume repeat business is. So I had to come up with something new to offer them besides oral sex. I just couldn't think of what to do. Until one night John asked me do something to him while we were having sex."

"We had just finished having normal sex and he was exhausted and spent. But I was still ready for more sex so he took out these plastic beads that were strung together and had me lube them and insert them in his ass. He then climbed back on top of me and started to thrust. He said he could go again but I had to do my part. John told me to slowly start to pull the string and take the beads out of his ass while we were screwing. It was amazing but he came again as soon as I started to pull them out. Now I knew what I could do to my clients to help them buy their liquid supplies from me."

Mei interjected that the beads were an old hooker's trick to make a client come. She did that when she had an older guy who would continue to screw her and not come. "After all, time is money" she said to the group.

"Thank you for that bit of information Mei" Doctor Willentz said sarcastically, "I appreciate your sharing that with the group."

"Yes" Barbara said. "A lot of my customers are older men and when I am blowing them they take forever sometimes. But if I have to screw them I can't spend all day with them. I started to use the beads and they really worked out well. And the old guys really appreciated it too."

"That was a helpful thing John taught me. Then one day I was late getting to his house after work, and I was very tired. I had to do a lot of driving in North Jersey and the stop and go traffic killed me. I didn't feel like doing anything with him that night. But he was in the mood and I told him I wasn't feeling very sexy that night."

"He walked into his closet and came out with these three small brass balls. They had a little weight to them, but not much. He lubed them and then had me slightly squat down a little. He pulled my thong to the side and started to insert them into my vagina. When they were all in he pulled my thong back up and had me stand straight. He said we were going to take a little walk down to the Hudson River and stroll along the promenade. He wasn't going to push sex on me, he said. But I had to keep those balls inside of me as I walked."

"I later learned they are called Ben Wa balls and they acted as a sexual stimulant as I walked along with him. They were really very pleasurable and I started to get excited as we took our time strolling along the water front that evening. It felt like someone was fingering me as I walked along and I had to use my vaginal muscles to also keep them in. By the time we got back to his place I was ready for him to start with me. Those stupid things really got me excited."

"That night was the start of his kinky sex with me. I didn't realize it then because I was truly in love with him. But as the weeks went on he started to get a little weirder, very slowly."

"First he asked if he could tie my hands and legs to the bed posts while he stimulated me. He had these Velcro bands and they were cushioned around my wrists and ankles. The other ends were put around his bed posts. I went along with it because I didn't know what he was going to do, but I decided to try it. He then put these clothes pin type of clamps on my nipples and it pinched and hurt a little, but I felt a tingling throughout my body. The oral sex that night literally drove me up a wall I was so excited. The restraints kept me from really moving and only heightened my orgasms."

"Then the next time he only tied my hands with Velcro to the posts on the headboard. I was on my knees bent over and face down on the bed. He took out a small fly swatter and gently hit my ass with it until it turned pink. While he did that he also stimulated me digitally until I was having a big orgasm. Then he entered me from the rear. But it eventually progressed to the point where I was getting hog tied on the floor and he was beating me until I came."

"I now realize he was into bondage and masochism but I didn't know it then. It was so gradual, and I really loved him and trusted him. Although I felt humiliated sometimes with the stuff he did to me I didn't stop it from happening. Like the odd things he inserted into me, I let him do it because I knew he cared for me. He used to put carrots and flashlights and even beer bottles in me, and I never refused him."

"One day he called me on my cell phone while I was working and said that that night we were going out to a club he used to go to all the time. I said okay as I was tired of just going to his place to hang out and have sex. He rarely took me out for dinner or a movie anymore so I was looking forward to that night."

"But I was in for a real surprise that evening. The club was in a rooftop penthouse at a hotel in Manhattan. It seems he belongs to a private member only S and M club. The club has a moving party each month in a different location where couples come and play sex games with each other. He pays over two hundred and fifty dollars a month to belong, but they hold it in very high end places."

"When I walked in most of the people there seemed to know John and waved hello to him when we entered. The men and women were all colors and sizes. The Asian women were on the petite side and the black men who were there were walking around totally nude exposing their massive manhood. Then I realized some of them were wearing leather outfits and the women were wearing even more bizarre outfits. There were whips lying about and ropes and all kinds of dildos with tubes of lube on the tables and buffets filled with food, booze and condoms."

"This was not going to be a normal party I thought, but I trusted John and didn't say anything to him about it. After all there was nothing there that he didn't already use on me so I felt comfortable walking in to that S and M party with him."

"He brought me a drink that he took from the bar and asked me to undress in front of everybody as they were all almost nude already. So I did it. When I was finished undressing I was standing in the living room with him, both of us totally naked, and people were just walking about drinking and feeling each other up. I felt a little uncomfortable, as I was the biggest woman there. Not that they were all skinny bitches but no one was as big as I was. Shit, I was standing there with my double G breasts just hanging there and as some of the women passed by they stopped to lick on them."

"John went back to the bar and got me another drink and then he put his arms around me and kissed me on the lips. That drink and the kiss on the lips calmed me down a lot and I started to relax a bit. But I should have known something was going to happen, it was just going too easy."

"The liquor was very strong and I suddenly felt tired. My large body mass must have blocked a lot of the booze from really knocking me out but I did feel kind of weak. Then the action started."

"Two of the other women who were totally undressed came over to me and the three of us were told to lie down on the carpet next to each other. I was in the middle of them. My wrists were tied to each of the women next to me on either side and my ankles were tied to them also. The three of us were now lying on the floor in a human chain tied down, and I was in the middle of it all."

"The girls on the sides of me turned towards me and we started to have a make out session together. They moved their hands all over me and I was unable to reciprocate. Yet I was starting to get really turned on by them."

"John then became the club leader and told the three of us to bend our knees upwards and two men held our wrists down on the floor behind our heads. Then the other women in the room kneeled down in front of us and started to take turns licking us until the three of us, tied together, were having an orgasm all at once. When all three of us were excited the men who were not holding our hands down knelt in front of us and took turns screwing us. I know that I did at least nine men that night vaginally. Then all the men helped the three of us up onto our knees and gently laid us down on our stomachs. At that point we were hit with their hands on our ass and the men who didn't get a chance to screw us before, screwed us in the ass."

"When everyone was finished with us, our hands were untied and we were told to get dressed. I was exhausted and humiliated. As John escorted me down to his car I couldn't even speak to him. Not that I was angry or something, but I was still tipsy and didn't really understand what had just happened."

"I do remember, as he was driving me back to his house and we were in the Holland Tunnel, that John told me I would soon remember this night. He said it was videotaped, and he would send me a copy of it before it went on the internet."

"How did you feel about that?" asked Doctor Willentz.

'It didn't bother me then. There was nothing that happened that I never did before, except for the number of men that had sex with me that night. I never had that many at one time. They treated me as a submissive slut and I didn't care. I was in love with John and I would have done anything he told me to do. I trusted him… and I loved him intensely, and the booze helped the situation along also" Barbara answered him.

"Are you still seeing him now?" asked Doctor Willentz.

"No. Not now. He drove me back to his house where I got into my car and drove home and went to sleep. Luckily I make my own hours because I didn't wake up for work until after noon the next day."

"I called him when I woke up but I got his answering machine so I figured he was at work."

Dawn asked her "what kind of work did he do?"

"I don't know, to be honest with you" replied Barbara.

"I never thought to ask. I figured whatever he did; he did it well enough to afford a three story house with an elevator only one block from the water in Edgewater. The homes in Edgewater New Jersey are not cheap."

"Anyway I then showered and washed away a ton of sperm that was still in me and had dripped down my legs while I slept. I had to douche twice just to clean myself out. Then I hung out at home in my nightgown trying to get rid of the headache I had from the drinks he gave me the previous night. I sat on my sofa and watched television. I didn't call him again until the following day when I went back to work."

"I tried to contact him all day with my cell phone but he never picked up. So after I made my sales calls I swung by his house on my way home to see him and maybe we'd go out for dinner together. But he was not home so I left. I drove home to have some dinner by myself. I stopped by a chicken place and picked up two ten piece buckets of crispy chicken and fries and brought it home to eat."

"The next few days I called him constantly but he never picked up. Then on the third day I called him after my first sales call of the day. I parked my car and dialed his number. There was a recorded message that his phone number was no longer in service. I immediately drove to his house and rang his door bell but there was no one home. I went next door and rang his neighbor's doorbell trying to find out where he was. This nice Asian lady came to the door and I asked her if she knew where John was, and did he leave any messages for me."

"She looked at me kind of funny and said there was no one by the name of John next door. His name was Charles and she did not know his last name. Anyway, she said, he moved out two days ago."

"I was devastated. The only man that ever showed me real attention and feelings just disappeared out of my life. He vanished into thin air. And then John wasn't his real name after all, I found out. I was devastated emotionally. I couldn't understand what had happened, what did I do to piss him off?"

Tears started to flow down her bulbous cheeks as she told the end of her story.

"That was a year ago, and I have never gotten over his leaving me. I get so depressed whenever I think about him. I truly miss him. I would have done anything he asked of me. Why, why did he leave me like that?"

She sobbed into a tissue. "I feel so used and discarded, like a disposable person."

"Barbara" Doctor Willentz asked, "Is that why you went to the bridge the other day? You wanted to end it all?"

Sobbing almost uncontrollably, she managed to say…"yes."

There was silence. Nobody said anything or even moved.

"Barbara" Doctor Willentz said to her, "he used you. You are a victim. He was never in love with you, but you were tricked into loving him. From your background it is apparent that you were easily manipulated by him. It is not your fault he took advantage of your feelings. There will be other people in your life who will love you for you. It is a big world out there and you will feel better as time goes on."

"I am not so sure" she answered him in a low trembling voice.

"Barbara" Doctor Willentz said, "you will see that time heals. He used you and played on your insecurities. There are men out there who like large women. I will bring you a list of the groups in Manhattan and New Jersey that cater to them and have weekly meet and greets. I am sure you will find a normal man who will love you regardless of what you think of yourself, and your negative self-image. There is a future for you of happiness."

"I will be setting aside some time for you next week when you are released. I would like to see you on a continuing basis to help you sort out your issues" he told her.

Barbara settled back in her chair and thanked him. She assured him she would follow up with him and keep that appointment.

Doctor Willentz turned from Barbara and spoke to the group. "I would like to thank Barbara for being honest with her emotions and feelings. It is getting late and they will be starting to serve dinner soon. Please go wash up quickly and we will meet in the hall way in five minutes and go together for dinner."

They all got up and went to their rooms and then gathered together shortly in the hallway to walk down the stairs for dinner. Barbara and Dawn waited upstairs for the elevator while the rest left. Barbara has knee problems from her weight and doesn't do stairs well.

While they were standing there Dawn turned to Barbara and said that she "was touched by her story" and if she ever wanted to talk to her privately she would be there for her.

"I know what it feels like not to have anyone to talk to" Dawn said to her. "I had many weeks alone while my husband was at work. Loneliness can be a terrible thing to experience" Dawn told her.

Barbara felt she was sincere and took Dawns hand into her pudgy fingers and gently pulled her towards her, and she kissed her on the cheek in gratitude.

When the elevator came they both walked in holding hands and smiling at each other.

Dinner

When the carts were brought into the dining room everyone was seated. Dinner that night was baked veal breaded with parmesan cheese instead of bread crumbs. The alternate dish was eggplant lasagna with a three cheese covering baked on. The side dish was French cut green beans in a vinaigrette soy sauce and small braised white potatoes tossed with seasoning.

Of course there was decaf coffee and tea, and plenty of clear sodas without caffeine.

For desert there was a baked apple crumb pie with vanilla ice cream on top if you wanted it.

Barbara had two helpings of the lasagna and three pieces of apple pie with plenty of ice cream on top.

Dawn sat between Mei and Barbara at the dinner table. When Barbara said she wanted another serving of lasagna but her knees were hurting her and she would have trouble getting up, Dawn was kind enough to get up and get it for her. Barbara smiled at Dawn and thanked her. She appreciated her helpfulness and kindness.

After dinner everyone was given some free time and they all got up. They either decided to walk outside in the garden or go back upstairs to read, watch television, or write a letter home. Barbara walked to the elevator to ring the elevator button to go up and Dawn went with her. They both stood next to each other waiting for the door to open.

When the elevator door finally opened they both walked in and the door closed. "You know" Barbara turned to Dawn and said, "That night at the club was my first lesbian experience. I never was with a woman before…to tell you the truth, it wasn't bad at all. I would do it again."

"I could tell" Dawn told her, as she took Barbara's hand in hers and gently kissed it. Barbara smiled at her. She was feeling wanted again.

Then the elevator reached the second floor and they both walked out and went to their own rooms to change into their night gowns.

The night nurse was sitting at her desk when the rest of the people came back from their walks and went to their rooms to change.

Shaniqua stopped by Barbara's room and peered in and asked her how she was doing tonight?

Barbara thought that was very kind of her to ask and thanked her for her thoughtfulness.

"Remember" Shaniqua told her "the Lord is there for you. Just ask and he will answer."

"Thank you. I will remember that" Barbara answered.

Barbara really didn't believe what she had just told her but she felt it would make Shaniqua feel better. "Why piss off someone if you don't have to" she thought to herself.

It was almost lights out and everyone was now in their rooms getting ready to settle in for the evening. They all had a small television in their room but by ten everything had to be turned off.

Dawn also had stopped by just before lights out and asked Barbara if she was doing okay after her talk that day. Barbara said she was feeling a little better and was sorry that Dawn couldn't stay with her a little longer.

Dawn asked her "would you really like me to stay with you tonight. If you do I can manage that."

"Yes, I feel like some hugs tonight" she answered Dawn.

Dawn said she would be right back. She went to her room and bunched her blanket up as if she were sleeping under it and took her spare nightgown and stuffed the arm with her towel and placed it over the blanket.

As ten o'clock approached the night nurse got up to make her rounds. She would walk by and open the door and peak in to make sure everyone was in their bed. If there was no light coming out from under the door sometimes she didn't bother to open it and just walked by.

After the night nurse had passed her Dawn had quietly walked back into Barbara's room and climbed into bed between her and the wall. Barbara was so big that when the night nurse opened the door and looked in, she didn't notice anything unusual.

Barbara turned to face Dawn and whispered that she was glad she came back. She missed her.

Dawn smiled at her, and perched on her elbow, Dawn leaned over towards Barbara and they kissed. Barbara's huge breasts slipped out of her robe and rubbed against Dawn's face as Dawn started to fondle and suck on them.

Barbara was thrilled that someone went out of their way to be with her, even if it was a girl. That Dawn had shown interest in her as a person impressed Barbara. Unconsciously she was transferring her affections for John to Dawn.

As a sexually submissive person Barbara let Dawn have her way with her that night. She spread her massive legs as Dawn stretched over Barbara's inner thigh with her hand, allowing it to reach in and stimulate her manually.

Dawn told Barbara to follow her lead and Barbara's massively pudgy hand slowly reached over between Dawn's legs and easily found its goal; and then gradually her thick middle finger entered Dawn's body. Her finger was so outsized that to Dawn it felt like a man was entering her and she started to experience an orgasm immediately.

After both of them had sexually exhausted themselves Dawn reached up and took Barbara's head in her hands. Dawn gently turned Barbara's head towards her and kissed her good night on her lips and then climbed out of her bed.

Dawn gingerly opened the door trying not to make any noise and looked to see if the coast was clear. Very softly she walked back to her room and climbed into her bed and tried to go to sleep.

Only a few minutes later Dawn heard some noise coming from her door.

"Psst, Psst" Mei was whispering as she opened Dawns door peeking in.

She quickly entered the room and tip toed over to Dawns bed and climbed in with her.

"Are you up?" she very quietly whispered as she softly started to kiss her on her neck.

Dawn turned over to face her, and answered her by sliding down in her bed and spreading Mei's legs apart as she did to Barbara.

There were no other words spoken that night as the two of them tightly intertwined their naked bodies with each other, and with the help of a hairbrush handle brought each other to climax numerous times.

Finally Mei left about an hour later to go to her room and Dawn, fully satisfied and exhausted, fell into a very deep sleep.

When the morning nurse made her rounds waking everyone up Dawn was still fatigued and wanted to sleep a little more. But she knew she had to get up.

The breakfast cart was in the hallway and the nurse brought in a hot cup of coffee to try to wake her up.

Groggily she got out of bed, put on a robe without doing her hair or makeup, quickly put on her slippers, and walked into the hallway to get a breakfast tray.

Everyone was out of their rooms now and getting their breakfast. They were slowly finding a spot to sit down and eat.

Doctor Willentz came walking in and he also took a tray and joined the group for breakfast.

When everyone was done he asked that they all return to their rooms to freshen up and be back in thirty minutes to get started with their therapy.

Dawn went back to her room and quickly fell asleep again.

Shaniqua helped the kitchen staff stack the empty trays on the cart as she was already dressed and ready. Getting up early for kitchen duty when she was working in the hotel kitchen was nothing new to her. By sunrise she was already dressed and waiting in the lounge watching the early news shows.

Finally everyone was out of their rooms and they walked over to the circle of chairs and took their seats. After the first few days they were all used to sitting in the same places.

Doctor Willentz started the conversation.

"Good morning, everyone" Doctor Willentz said. "I hope we are all rested and ready to begin. As you might have realized we are nearing the end of our week together and it's time to start seeing how we can help each other."

Chapter Eight - Day Four

"I would like to start today's session by asking if anyone has any questions or thoughts they would like to bring up to the group" Doctor Willentz asked.

Jose raised his hand and started to speak. "I was thinking about what Doctor Willentz said to me about Maribel leaving me. Maybe it wasn't my fault, but I still feel depressed over it. Why do I still feel that way"?

"Emotions" Doctor Willentz answered, "are a hard thing to overcome. It is a hard wired brain function, in layman's term, and we just have to accept that it hurts but as time moves on you will replace her with someone else. In the meantime I have a prescription for some medication that will help you to some degree. I will give it to you when you leave here tomorrow."

"I can understand his emotional breakdown" Shaniqua chimed in. "I am here because I had a similar experience emotionally, but it dealt with death. I was so depressed I could not get out of bed. It hurts. It really hurts inside… and all you want is for it to end."

"Shaniqua" Doctor Willentz answered, "yes, what you felt was an emotional loss very similar to Jose'. But you both have the rest of your lives to live and there are good things that can be ahead of both of you."

"Your baby will bring you the love that you need to carry on. It will be a reminder of Eric and the hope and future that you both had envisioned for yourselves. This baby will be the thing you need to focus your thoughts on. You need to protect and nurture it. To bring you back from depression and to restart your life.

It won't be easy but it can be done" Doctor Willentz told her in a reassuring tone.

Dawn sat there silently. She did not agree with what he had said about forgetting an old love. That talk by Doctor Willentz triggered her to remember when her first son was born with William. How that birth reminded her of Christopher, the baby she gave away for adoption on Christmas Day. A rush of memories flooded her thoughts. Marcus' face flashed before her eyes and she began to relive that night in the back seat of his car in her mind's eye. She heard the music from the car radio, the smell of his breadth as they held each other, and the thrill of her first sexual encounter.

"No", she said to the group, "you don't forget. It becomes duller as time moves on but it can come roaring back at certain times. Especially for me at Christmas, that's when I gave birth and lost my son to some unknown family. I will never forget my first baby."

Taking a deep breath Dawn sat upright in her chair and looked around at the group. She surprised herself at her assertiveness but decided not to continue talking and to sit quietly and listen. It hurt too much to continue to talk about it again.

Doctor Willentz heard what she said but did not push her to delve deeper into her feelings at that moment. He felt there was not enough time and hopefully he could meet with her privately later in the day.

Mei" Doctor Willentz said, "Are there any thoughts you would like to contribute to the group today?"

"Not really" she said in a sort of cavalier tone of voice. "I am going back to work for Semmi when I get out of here. And I know that Eddie will be there for me also. I just have to stay on my meds and stay off crack. Then I'll be okay, I guess."

"I understand" Doctor Willentz answered. "But isn't there something else you would like to do for a living? Maybe go back to school? Get married? Have what many people consider a normal lifestyle, he asked her."

"Doc" Mei answered, "I have been doing this for many years now and it's the only thing I know how to do, and I do it well. And Semmi gives me a big cut of the money I earn. It's more than the other girls get."

Mei continued. "I live in a new penthouse with Semmi on Park Avenue; have a chauffeured driver and bodyguard when I do outcalls, and there isn't anything I want that I can't buy or have someone buy for me."

"Plus I have Eddie for when I feel the need to be wanted by a man, and not just for sex" she told him.

Doctor Willentz answered her that he understood how she felt and if she feels mentally well enough about it, then there is nothing he can do right now. But if she should have second doubts in the future to please contact him and he will immediately see her for a consultation.

Mei thanked him and sat back in her chair again, content with his answers.

Amanda raised her hand to speak and she was acknowledged.

"I know I follow some men… but I really don't think I am a stalker. They led me on and I just wanted to see if they changed their mind, that's all I did" she explained.

"But the law" Doctor Willentz started to explain to her, "says that what you did is considered stalking. If someone says they don't want to see you anymore you have to let it go. You can't force someone to love you" he told her.

“I know” she answered him, “but I can’t help myself. I just have to see them again. I feel that maybe they will change their minds.”

“Amanda” Doctor Willentz said to her, “the next time you get caught stalking the judge is going to lock you up for a long time, possibly in a mental hospital. I would suggest that you come back to see me on an outpatient basis when you leave here.”

“Yer, I guess I will” she replied. But she really didn’t mean it. She said it to settle the discussion.

Barbara was the last one.

Doctor Willentz looked at her as she sat quietly on her chair.

At that moment the lunch cart came in and they stopped and went to get something to eat.

Lunch

As the cart was wheeled in Barbara stood up and slowly moved towards it with her flabby inner thighs chafing as she walked. She picked up an egg salad sandwich on fresh rye bread and two bags of baked potato chips and a sweetened ice tea. Her tray was almost full but she was able to slide a plate of chocolate cake onto it also. Carefully she walked over to the table where she always sat and started to eat her lunch.

The others also walked over to the cart except for Mei. She had other things on her mind and was not interested in food right then. She was thinking of Dawn and how she might be able to see her again after they both leave the institute. She knew Dawn would never leave her kids to enter the business full time, but maybe part time, she thought.

Lunch was a little longer than usual as Doctor Willentz wanted to speak to Mei privately.

The doctor decided that maybe he would have better luck with Mei if he sat with her during lunch and they had a brief but candid conversation.

"Do you mind if I sit here today with you" he asked before sitting down. He was already sitting down when the question was asked and she had no time to really answer.

"No. I guess it's alright" Mei responded to him.

As he stirred his coffee he looked at her and spoke very softly but directly at her.

"Mei, you are a very young girl with a lot of life experiences already" he told her. "And not all of it is good or even healthy… both mentally and physically" he told her.

"Being here is your opportunity to change the direction your life is in. I am here to help you" he told her before pausing. "If you want it" he concluded saying to her.

Mei looked up at him and smiled. Slowly she leaned over to him so only he could hear her and she began to speak in a very soft voice.

"I never finished high school and I have no skills other than my body to make a living with. I live in a penthouse in Manhattan, have all the nice clothes and expensive jewelry I want, make more money in one year than you will ever make and I do it just by spreading my legs apart."

"As long as I can do it, I will. Semmi had me open a brokerage account under an assumed name" she continued, "and no one will ever trace that money to me. But it is there if I ever need it. And I want to tell you it is a lot of money. So no, I will never stop doing what I am doing as long as I have the ability to do it" Mei confidently told him.

She smiled coyly at him, then sat back in her chair and waited for him to answer her.

Doctor Willentz picked up his coffee cup and took a few light sips, then sat back and thought of his answer to her.

"Mei" he said, "you are right. Everything you said is truthful and I have no answers to anything you mentioned. But it will eventually wear you down, if not kill you. Think about how many girls live to a ripe old age doing what you do. How many die young due to either violence or disease. This is your opportunity to turn your life around" he concluded telling her.

She listened, smiled at him, thanked him for his concerns and efforts, then sat back in her chair and waited till tomorrow when she would be leaving.

Realizing it was a losing battle Doctor Willentz finished his coffee and told her that he would always be available to her if she ever needed him. He reached into his jacket pocket and took out one of his business cards and gave it to her.

Mei took it and placed it in her robe pocket, and quickly forgot it was there. She never even looked at it.

He stood up, thanked her for listening to him, and called everyone back to the circle to finish that afternoons session.

Once they were all seated he turned his attention to Barbara and asked her how she was feeling emotionally.

"Well, since I have been here I have met some very caring people who I became friends with. I hope to continue our friendship after I leave tomorrow" she answered.

"But yes, I felt deeply betrayed by John, or Charles or whatever his name is. I felt wanted by him and when he abandoned me I went out of my mind with a feeling of total loss. It felt to me almost like a death occurred… to someone I deeply cared about and trusted" Barbara said.

"That is not an unusual feeling" Doctor Willentz told her. "But killing yourself is not the answer. When you do that you only hurt yourself, not him. Obviously he couldn't care less about what you do to yourself. But the people here do care and we want you to have a full life, not a short one."

Barbara replied that she understood what he was saying and that she now realizes that she almost made a terrible mistake.

Being satisfied with that answer Doctor Willentz ended the group early and said that he arranged for a movie to be brought in for them that night. It was just released on DVD and he brought it for them to see.

He said he would see them all at dinner and they were free to walk the grounds this afternoon as they wished.

As he left to go to the elevator Dawn and Mei walked with Barbara to the corner of the room to sit and talk together about their future plans after they leave the institute tomorrow.

The three of them had developed an emotional friendship and were anxious to get together after they left here.

Dawn asked the two of them if they wanted to visit her next week after William went to work. William had put the children into a nursery school when Dawn was admitted and she would now have the days free to entertain them in her apartment.

Mei said she would have to check her schedule but Tuesdays were her day off and she thought she would be available late morning. It all depended on what went on Monday night. She told them that "if Tuesdays were not good I'll see what I could do. After all I do work nights."

Barbara said she was sure she could make it. She had to get her car from the impound lot on Monday and would love to see Dawn's apartment. As she made her own hours as a traveling salesperson it was not a problem for her to shift things around so she could meet both of them.

Amanda had walked down the back steps to go outside for some fresh air when she met a male staff nurse on the first floor. She stopped to talk to him before she got out of the building. He was a more mature man in his thirties which she always found attractive. The young guys just did not do anything for her. They exchanged phone numbers after a few minutes talking and she asked him to join her at the movie that night, since he was on staff. As he looked her over he felt that she was available, so he took her hand and they walked outside by some tall bushes; where he then turned and kissed her. He knew it was wrong to do that with a patient but she was very attractive and had her top buttons open on her hospital gown.

As they embraced he pulled her close and felt her warm body rubbing against his. While they kissed passionately his hands roamed all over her body. Finally they both decided to lie on the soft grass as she pulled her gown up over her waist and initiated intercourse.

Upstairs Shaniqua went back to her room to read a book she had loaned from the institute library and to just have some quiet time to herself. She sat and rubbed her stomach as she was now showing. She had decided to buy some maternity clothes that weekend when she went home.

Jose just sat and watched television by himself. He was withdrawn and had no plans for when he left.

Chapter Nine - Evening

Everyone that evening came back and took a chair and faced the television that was hanging on the wall. The movie was going to start soon.

The evening nurse came in with the cart carrying the DVD, and hooked the wires to the television then started the DVD player, turned the lights down a little, and the movie started.

Dawn, Mei and Barbara sat in the back and when the lights went down they held hands while watching the movie.

After it was playing a bit Amanda got up and said she was going to the bathroom and walked away. She turned quickly into her room and the male nurse was waiting there for her.

He opened her gown and fondled her while she put her hand down his scrubs and touched him. He was quickly aroused.

Amanda knelt on the floor and instantly pulled his pants down and put him in her mouth. He stood there moaning silently as she finished him off.

When she was done she left her room and walked back to the group and sat down to watch the ending of the movie.

What the male nurse did not know was that Amanda had now set her sights on him. She fully intended to hook up with him after she left the institute.

The male nurse blissfully walked out of the room and walked the other way, and left the ward. He was soon to find out what he had started, Amanda would finish.

The lights were turned on when the movie was over and everyone stood up and walked back to their rooms for the night.

Chapter Ten - Day Five

The breakfast cart was brought in and as it was Doctor Willentz walked in to the ward and asked everyone to please fill out a questionnaire after breakfast that he had to send to the sponsoring foundation for the grant.

Doctor Willentz already knew the answers to the questionnaires. He felt that there was not enough time for it to be meaningful but he had to hand them out anyway and send them in.

He announced that after breakfast he would like to meet with everyone individually for a few minutes in the ward office before they left.

He felt very badly that he could not do enough for them and he knew they really needed more time together to be effective. But he had to finish the week as best he could.

One by one they came in to see him and after a few minutes each was able to leave the institute. A car service was brought in to take each person to their home if they did not have a ride. He had that list of addresses and after they got dressed in street clothes they were individually escorted downstairs to the lobby to await their ride.

The social worker at the institute went during the week to the mall in Paramus and bought Barbara some clothes that would fit her; so she could leave in street clothes.

When Mei was escorted to the lobby a large white Cadillac Escalade was waiting for her.

Min-Jun quickly walked around and opened the rear door for Mei to enter as Semmi was waiting in the rear seat for her. They embraced, kissed, and the Cadillac drove away to Manhattan.

William came to pick up Dawn and he embraced her in the lobby and was glad she was coming home. She kidded him, smiled and walked quickly with him to his car.

The others relied on the car service limo that Doctor Willentz hired to take them home.

After everyone had left Doctor Willentz went into his office and sat down to write a letter to the foundation that had given him the grant to try this experiment.

The previous night while the group was watching the movie he had dinner with the head of the Rachmunitz foundation. The foundation was the one who gave the Institute the grant to try this short term approach. They had discussed the process and the results of the week and they both reached the same conclusion.

But Doctor Willentz had to send him a written report based on the group's written form that he handed out. He was also going to give his opinion and ask for a longer process grant.

Doctor S. Willentz
The Willentz Institute
675 Institute Road
Bergan County NJ

Mr. Mazel Rachmunitz
The Rachmunitz Chai Foundation
1818 Main Line Avenue
Perth Amboy N.J.08861

Dear Mazel,

It was a pleasure to see you last night at dinner and talk about the short term project your foundation sponsored on an experimental basis.

I am sorry to say I feel that it did not help everyone who participated as much as we had hoped for.

As discussed I feel that it was a valiant effort but either there were too many people involved or we needed more time to fully explore their problems.

I will follow up with the patients within the next few weeks and see if they need any more help, which I am sure they do.

Dealing with assorted mental and real addictions in one week, I feel, is not enough time.

In a follow up letter to come a more fully detailed account of the results will be sent to you.

Again, thank you.
Doctor S. Willentz

Chapter Eleven - Follow up - Dawn

It was now Monday morning and Dawn had spent the weekend at home with William and the children.

Saturday they all went to a local park and the kids played on the playground while William sat next to Dawn and watched them play, and they had a quiet conversation together.

"Dawn" William asked, "Do you feel that the institute helped you any?"

"Yes" she answered. "I met some new friends who also had personal problems, but of a different kind. We became very close friends in our short time there."

She continued "I don't feel that I have to drink anymore; and I am going to start a 12 step program as Doctor Willentz suggested. I have a meeting on Monday night that he found for me, right here in town. I plan on going to it. Can you come early to watch the kids?"

"Yes" he answered. "I'm glad that you are on the road to recovery. I missed you very much" he told her as he held her hand in his, smelling the perfume on her neck as it drifted toward him with the slight wind that was blowing in the park.

He leaned over to her and softly kissed her on her neck.

Afterwards the family went for hot dogs and soda and then they drove over to visit Dawns mother for her to see the children.

William had a new Cadillac and the kids were put into their car seats in the rear and Dawn sat in the front with William.

She took her hand and rubbed it on the leather seats as she smelled that new car odor as they went to see her mom.

That first week home flew by and Dawn did her house cleaning and food shopping herself. She also stopped by her mother's house with the kids for a quick visit with her on Thursday.

She took the kids to daycare nursery school and the oldest one to preschool every day before she went back home for breakfast.

Saturday was a very uneventful day for her.

On Sunday Dawn woke up very early before daybreak and took the laundry basket down to the basement where the washing machines were.

She left the apartment and took the elevator down to the basement where the laundry room was.

Although she had a large condo there was no room for a washer and dryer so she still had to go to the basement.

As she was loading the dirty clothes into the machine she heard a familiar voice greet her hello.

Dawn turned around and there was Kathy walking in with some young man holding her laundry basket.

"Hi Dawn, how are you doing?" Kathy said in an extremely friendly tone of voice. "I heard you were away for a while. I missed you" Kathy told her as she kissed her on the lips.

Dawn returned the kiss, and smiled at her as she stepped back to continue putting her laundry into the washer.

"Yes, I went to a rehab for my drinking and the pills I was taking" she told her. "I'm clean now and I want to stay that way. No more booze or drugs for me. I can't handle that stuff anymore" she told her.

"I understand" Kathy replied.

"But I have to tell you that your videos are very hot and they are selling like mad. I was interviewed the other day in a club in Manhattan by a reporter for the porn trade paper and he told me you were up for best porn actress of the year!"

"I don't understand" Dawn replied. What awards? I didn't know there were even such things."

"Dawn, your videos are selling out everywhere they are sold. And the internet is flaming out over them also. I am making a lot of money from them and the distributors want more videos with you in them" Kathy continued telling her.

"But I can't do the drugs anymore. I can't handle the schedule you had me on. I was exhausted doing them all day and then having to watch the kids when I got home. I don't know if I can do anymore for you" she told Kathy.

Not wanting to lose a good thing Kathy made her a great offer.

"Dawn, I can arrange a half day shoot twice a week instead of doing it all in one day or even two full days like we used to. If we have to carry over to the next week we can. This way you get to rest and you can still make good money."

Kathy continued trying to sell her on the idea.

"I can now pay you more because your videos are very hot. I will pay you ten thousand dollars a video, in cash, if you agree to come back to work for me" she explained to Dawn.

"Let me think about it and I'll get back to you on Monday Dawn told her.

Kathy was satisfied with that answer and had her young boy toy put her laundry in the washing machine for her.

She kissed Dawn goodbye and then she left holding her boy toy's hand.

Dawn stayed in the laundry room while her clothes were in the dryer. When it was finished she took it all out and folded everything. Then she packed up her clean laundry into her basket and went back upstairs to her condo to sort it and put it away.

On the elevator ride upstairs Dawn began to think of the things she could buy with that kind of money.

If she continued doing the porn movies she wouldn't be dependent on William giving her money to spend. Her mind started to race and dream of all sorts of things she could buy.

With the money she had made before with Kathy she opened a safe deposit box in the bank down the block, and she kept all of it in there. It was almost all still there. She was very stingy spending it.

Dawn hid one of the keys to the vault box behind her makeup table by using gaffing tape to hold it. Then she put the other one in her closet taped over the transom on the inside of the closet. She was sure nobody would see it there as there were no lights in her small closet.

After six months of making porn movies she had accumulated a lot of cash in the bank box and would soon need a larger one. She had been cranking out movies at the rate of three every two weeks. Besides being exhausted she had a lot of hidden money.

But this time she could make a lot more money and it would be easier on her both physically and mentally. And not as time consuming, she thought.

But she wanted to speak to someone else about it. Someone who she felt would be truthful with her.

When she walked back into the apartment William was still sleeping, as it was still early on a Sunday morning. She walked as quietly as she could so as not to wake anyone and she put the laundry basket down by the side of her sofa. Dawn took her cell phone and went out onto her balcony that was overlooking Manhattan as the sun was just coming up over the horizon.

She felt that Mei would give her an honest answer. She dialed her and waited for it to ring.

"Hi Dawn" Mei said. "It's great to hear from you so soon."

Her caller ID let her know who was calling her. Mei never answered blocked calls for security reasons. She wanted a record of who called so it could be traced if she was ever kidnapped or in danger.

"I hope I'm not disturbing you, or waking you. I know it's early and you were probably out last night" Dawn told her.

"No, it's okay. I just got in. I'm at Eddie's place now. He picked me up after I was finished with my last appointment at the Empire Hotel on Madison" Mei responded.

"Listen, I have a question for you" Dawn said. "I'm not sure what to do. Kathy wants me to make more videos and is offering me ten thousand dollars a video. And I don't have to make as many either."

"Really" Mei said. "That sounds great."

"Also" Mei continued "I just heard that you are up for porn actress of the year. I saw your picture in one of Semmi's porn magazines. The newspapers are looking for you for interviews, but they can't find you."

"Even TMI is on the lookout for you. They have the paparazzi all over Manhattan going into the clubs just waiting for you to show up. But I know you don't go clubbing."

Dawn was flustered. She did not expect this, nor did she want it. The silence was broken as Mei told her that her secret was safe with her.

Again there was silence.

Dawn for the first time began to realize that the life she has with William could be jeopardized. She knew he would definitely leave her and also take the kids. He had no idea she was a world famous porn star and now she had a real quandary to work out.

"Mei" Dawn said, "I am not sure that this is what I want. I just did it because I was bored and it was a little extra spending money for me. I really don't want to lose my family over this."

"I don't know what to tell you" Mei responded to her.

"You are talking about big money now" she said to her. You can play this thing up and wind up making millions in the porn industry. Plus the endorsements could be tremendous. This can be a really huge opportunity for you."

"Ok, let me think about this a little bit more. I am not really sure what to do right now. I'll call you back when I decide. And thanks for keeping my secret."

"Not a problem" Mei said. "I'll talk to you soon".

Dawn turned around and went back inside and sat down at her kitchen table. She stared out the large picture window at the sun rising over Manhattan and didn't move.

She was confused and her mind was racing now as to what should she do.

Finally the thought came to her to call her friend Annette Marie that she grew up with in Maplewood. Dawn realized where Mei was coming from and she wasn't satisfied with her advice. Annette, she felt, would be more level headed and down to earth. They came from the same background and she felt more comfortable with the advice she would give her.

Slowly she dialed her number, not sure how to really start this conversation. When they were younger she was a mousey flat chested little girl that none of the boys thought of dating. Now that she was a porn star everyone wanted to screw her. Her problem was should she walk away from her husband and kids for fame and money.

“Hello Annette, this is Dawn” she said into her cell phone. “How are you?”

“Dawn, is this really you?” Annette answered. I haven’t heard from you in a long time. How have you been? I missed talking to you. How are the kids?”

“Oh, they are fine” she answered. “But I have a real problem and I need good advice.... I know you will give me an honest answer.”

“Sure Dawn, you know I will always be there for you” answered Annette.

“Well here is my problem. After the three kids were born William was putting in more hours at his company trying to expand the business. I was home alone with the three kids and I was bored. Plus the fact that William is much older than me and his sex drive isn’t enough to satisfy me.”

“So I met his lady in my building that makes porn movies and she asked me to help out in one. She paid me a lot of money and the guys I was having sex with were young, great looking guys that in high school wouldn’t even look at me. Now they are screwing me and I’m getting paid for it”.

“But I recently had to go to a rehab for pills and booze and now I’m clean. This morning I saw the movie lady and she offered me even more money than I was making before. “

“She also said I’m in demand as a porn star.”

“I’m up for some industry award or something. Plus the paparazzi are looking for me. If I do more movies I'll lose William and my kids, but I'll be able to make some really big money and endorsements and stuff. I don't know what to do, that's why I'm calling you."

There was silence on the phone. Annette couldn't believe that the girl she grew up with was now a porn queen. She really did not know what to say to her.

Finally Annette was able to make some sense of the facts that she was told. And she decided to be very open and honest with Dawn.

"If I were you" she told Dawn, "I would try to keep my family together. You can always have an affair on the side and no one will find out. But I don't think it's worth losing your home and kids over this. You don't need the money and why lose everything over this" she concluded.

Then she hit her with the line that really closed the deal on her thoughts.

"Remember how you felt when you gave Christopher up for adoption when you were in high school" she told her. "Do you want to go through a messy divorce and maybe lose your three kids also?"

"I couldn't bear to do that. It would kill me" Dawn answered her. Now she knew she had her answer for Kathy.

She thanked Annette for her insight and when William woke up an hour later she asked him to take care of the kids for a few minutes while she went to speak to a neighbor in the building.

The elevator ride up was pretty quick but seemed very slow to her now. She had to turn down a chance to be a real star.

When Kathy answered the door she smiled and asked Dawn to come in, but she declined.

"I can't chance losing my family doing this anymore" she told her in the doorway. "It's too much for me to risk, and I am sorry."

"I understand" Kathy replied. "I am sorry to lose you, but you never know what the future may bring. Someday if you change your mind call me."

With that said Dawn thanked her again for the opportunity and went back down stairs to her condo and her family.

When she entered her apartment she kissed William on the lips and told him she loved him. He smiled and didn't know what to make of this. She never did this before to him.

He slowly sat down at the kitchen table to read the newspaper and Dawn took her cell phone and walked out onto the balcony to make another phone call.

"Hello Mei, this is Dawn."

"Hi Dawn, what's up?"

"I turned down that movie offer" she told her. "But I need the sex. If you have any really good looking guys on a weekday while my kids are in school, and you need another girl, let me know in advance… okay? I'd appreciate it, and I'd be willing to help out if the money was good and he had stamina. I just can't be in the movies with all that fame stuff. But I still need the sex, though. Call me if I can help you out."

"That's great" Mei said. "I have plenty of daytime calls but Semmi's girls are usually tired from the evenings work. I'll tell her and she'll make all the arrangements."

"By the way, I'm going to be in Jersey next week. I'll stop by and we can spend some time together" Mei told her.

"I'd love that" Dawn said. "See you next week."

When Dawn hung up with Mei she decided to visit the beauty parlor down the street on Tuesday since they are closed on Mondays. She was going to have her long hair cut very short and also dyed blond to change her look. She couldn't afford to have her picture plastered all over the newspapers. She was hoping that the paparazzi wouldn't recognize her if they ever found out where she lived.

Chapter Twelve - Follow up - Mei 메이

Semmi picked her up from the Willentz Institute and they drove back to Manhattan to the penthouse she owned.

Mei was happy to be back with Semmi and they kissed and fondled each other as they drove over the George Washington Bridge towards Manhattan.

Once they were on the West Side Highway Semmi started to ask about Mei's week at the Institute.

"There were six of us in a group therapy thing" Mei told her. "We sat around in a kind of circle and we each spoke about how we got there, and some suggestions were made as to how we can get better."

“I just had to get the drugs out of my system. I’m not sure the week I was there is enough. They gave me something to counter the coke and I feel a lot better now, but not great” she revealed her.

“The doctor spoke to me about getting out of the business but I enjoy it and I could not leave you under any circumstances” Mei said as she laid her head onto Semmi’s lap.

Gently Semmi stroked her hair as the car turned off the highway. “You are my goyanj-i” [kitten] Semmi whispered to her. “We will be together forever”.

Semmi over the years had mentally become her mother and looked upon Mei as the child she never had, besides being her lover. There was this strange kind of bond that developed between them that became stronger over the years.

As Min-jun finally arrived at their building he turned into the driveway and pulled in to their assigned parking spot.

He turned off the SUV and ran around to open the door for them to get out. Min-jun offered his hand to help Semmi step down; then he escorted them to the private elevator in the rear of the parking garage.

When the elevator door opened they walked into a private lobby and Semmi pressed the security panel with her combination to unlock the front door. As it opened Mei saw Eddie and the elderly woman waiting for them to enter. They all hugged and kissed and were very happy to see Mei again.

Semmi had ordered food to be brought in from one of her Korean restaurants that she owned. So when they were all finished greeting Mei they followed Semmi into the dining area and sat down to a delicious meal.

She had arranged for Choon Chun Makgooksu (with broth) to start the meal. Then there was also on the table Gochang Eel BBQ, Jeju Black Pig BBQ, and finally Hoengsung Hanwoo (Korean Beef) cooked just perfectly. The old lady had prepared Daegu Flat Dumplings herself and she brought them from Queens to share with everyone.

When they were finished eating everyone stood up with full stomachs and walked slowly into the living room to sit down and hear about Mei's experiences last week at the Institute.

Both Eddie and Semmi missed her a lot, and both were in love with her. Eddie knew he had to go easy with his feelings for Mei because Semmi owned her, and she didn't mind sharing, but would not tolerate losing her.

When everyone had left the table Min-jun and the two chefs were allowed to sit there and finish what was left over, which was a lot of great food.

Two scantily dressed Korean girls in their twenties brought out bottles of wine, and glasses for everyone, to toast Mei's return home.

As they all sat back Mei started to tell about the people who were there. She told them their stories but held back certain things that were mentioned that she thought were not fair game to share.

Mei mentioned that Doctor Willentz had spoken to her about leaving Semmi and Eddie but she said she could not do that to the people that she cared about. As soon as Mei had said that Semmi stood up and walked over to her and embraced her; and they started to kiss. Semmi told everyone that she missed her goyanj-i and with that took Mei by the hand and led her to the bedroom where they would be for the next hour or so.

Eddie knew better than to say anything so he sat there silently watching television. The old lady knew what to do and signaled to the two Korean waitresses. She spoke to them in Korean and said they were to take Eddie to one of the side bedrooms and entertain him.

The two girls walked over to Eddie and each girl took one of his hands and they escorted him to the side bedroom; where they soon all undressed and laid down on the bed to start their orgy of lust.

When Semmi and Mei had finished they were in each other's arms on the bed gently kissing each other. Semmi whispered to Mei that she knew Eddie had feelings for her, and she did too. It would be okay if she were to be with him, and even marry him. She knew that someday Mei might want to have children and Eddie was a hardworking man and had a respectable job. Plus he didn't mind that Mei worked for Semmi.

She was trying to hold onto her lover in a way that would prevent her from someday leaving her altogether. It was okay for her to have Eddie as long as Semmi was also in the picture. After all Mei was not only her lover but her trusted worker; and in Semmi's mind the future owner of her business. She would be willing to transfer everything to Mei just as the old lady had done for her. Mei was her retirement plan, but Mei did not know that yet. In the future she would get to run everything.

By the time Semmi and Mei walked out of the bedroom Eddie and the girls were already done and waiting for them to return.

Semmi turned to Eddie and took him by his hand as they walked into the kitchen to talk. She had some things to tell him.

"Eddie I like you. You and Mei and I have been together a few times and I know she likes you. If you would like to see more of her I am okay with it" she told him.

"Yes, I would like to see Mei more often but I don't want to interfere with you and her" he replied back. He knew that she was not to be fooled with. She was a dangerous woman to screw with. He had to be open with her or else he would be in a lot of trouble, and he knew it.

"Why don't you take Mei dancing tonight?" she suggested to him. "There's a new club downtown in the Wall Street area. It's in an office building on the top floor overlooking the bay. It's not a residential building so the noise doesn't bother anyone at night. I'll have Min-jun drive you two there now. Have a good time, see you."

Min-jun escorted them down stairs and he opened the door for them to get in. He hopped into the front passenger seat and they all drove down to the Wall Street area.

They went to the club and started to dance but they both felt like sitting and talking so they sat down on the side in a small booth. It was time to talk privately.

Mei remembered what Eddie had said when she almost jumped out of the window. The rest of that night was a little foggy to her; but that he said he loved her… she didn't forget that.

Other men had told her that but they were paying her so she knew where that was coming from. But Eddie wasn't paying her when he said that, and he did save her life.

Mei took his hand and pulled him close to her. "I have to tell you something Eddie" she said. "I feel very close to you, maybe even love you and I would like to see more of you. But I can't leave Semmi. I love her too, and I work for her also. If you can live with that situation then we can be together more often. Maybe I can even move in with you for a few days a week. It's up to you" she told him.

Eddie knew that was the best thing he would get from her at this time, so he agreed.

Mei was thrilled and pulled his head to hers and kissed him lightly and sexually, while grinding her body into his and feeling his arousal.

They decided to leave the club and Min-jun, who was waiting outside for them, drove them to Eddie's place where he dropped them off very early in the morning.

They went up to his apartment, off of Third Avenue, and walked right into the bedroom.

Eddie pulled the comforter down as they undressed and slid under the top sheet. They reached out to one another and embraced, and then they started to grope each other, when Mei's phone rang.

Mei sat up and told Eddie to wait a minute that she has to answer it, it could be business. She pressed the button to open her phone case and she saw on caller ID who it was.

"Hi Dawn" Mei said. "It's great to hear from you so soon…."

Chapter Thirteen - Follow up - Juan

As the limo entered the Lincoln Tunnel Juan was sitting in the back and thinking about how he was going to make a living.

He still had an apartment in Chelsea but he was behind on the rent and was awaiting an eviction notice from the landlord. In New York it takes up to six months to evict someone; so he knew he had some time yet before he was homeless.

When the limo pulled up to the curb next to his building he got out, thanked the driver, and went upstairs to sit and try to figure what was his next move in life.

He knew that he had to find some kind of a job or he would be out on the streets in a few months. So he decided to walk along the Ninth Avenue and see if there were any help wanted signs in the store front windows.

Every day for two weeks he walked the streets looking. He also walked into a few personnel agencies to see what kind of jobs they might have for him.

The agencies either had jobs for people with certain work backgrounds or they had general labor jobs in construction.

He was getting desperate looking for work. Finally he decided that maybe he would work as a male escort since he was bisexual he could date either ladies or men.

He knew that in Times Square there were a lot of men handing out flyers for escorts but they all looked kind of seedy to him. Juan didn't feel comfortable calling those services to work for them. But he thought maybe if he reached out to Mei she might be able to help him.

It was a few weeks after they had all left the Institute when he called her.

"Hi Mei, this is Juan. We were at the Institute together. How are you doing?" he asked her.

She didn't have his phone number in her contacts so she was taken off guard when he called. Her phone ID didn't pop up with his name.

"Okay, how are you?" she replied back to him.

"I'm having a hard time making ends meet. I was wondering if you ever needed a male escort?" he told her.

"Yes, as a matter of fact Semmi is starting one up soon. We are looking for good looking men. Can don't you stop by our office for an interview tomorrow? I'll text you the address when we hang up. Figure about two in the afternoon. I'll see you then" Mei told him.

"Great, thank you. I appreciate it."

Then he put his phone away and went back to his apartment to look for clean clothing and press his best looking suit so it wasn't wrinkled.

Juan was a handsome man, on the thin side, but was still very handsome. He was just a little tired looking from life screwing him over a bit. But he was determined to make a good impression tomorrow and realized this might be an opportunity for him to make some money.

The next day he left his apartment and started to walk over to Semmi's office which was in her condo. He easily found the building and approached the door man to ring upstairs that he was here.

Bea Jacobs spoke to the doorman and Juan was walked to the elevator by the doorman where he was asked to wait. Juan was told that Bea would send someone down to escort him up stairs.

When the elevator door opened a beautiful young black girl in a tight fitting sweater and jeans was standing in it. She asked if he was Juan. When he said he was she motioned for him to come in and she introduced herself to him and they went upstairs together to meet Semmi.

When the elevator stopped they walked out and into a private lobby with only one entry door. She rang and a young Chinese girl in a red tight fitting dress with a slit going up the dress on the side, to her thigh, opened it and greeted them as they entered.

Semmi was sitting on the sofa and stood up to greet Juan. Mei had told her about him and she was eager to meet with him. She knew that he had experience in the fashion business and knew a lot of key people in that world.

Semmi did too, but introductions to Semmi was like money, you never have too much.

She motioned for him to sit down on the sofa with her; and the other two girls left the room and sat with Bea in her office helping on the phones.

They discussed they state of the fashion industry and they both dropped names of people that they knew trying to see if there were and connections they both knew. Luckily for Juan there was and Semmi was satisfied with his answers and presentation.

She knew he could go both ways but he would have to be trained so he knew what to say, how to act, and be a reliable escort for her.

Semmi called the black girl back out from the office and told Juan that Yaashika would be his supervisor. She will teach him what he needed to know and she would be his contact in the future.

Yaashika told gave Juan her business card with her cell number on it and told him she was to contact her exclusively, not Mei, if he had any questions.

Juan agreed and took the card and put it in his suit pocket.

"Okay then" Yaashika said, "We have to go shopping. I want you to have a few suits and blazers and be able to represent us appropriately."

Juan turned to Semmi and thanked her for the opportunity and he and Yaashika left the apartment and went downstairs.

When they got to the lobby they walked out onto the street and Min-Jun was waiting by the SUV to drive them both to Soho to get him clothes.

The hip men's stores there were full of pricey highly styled clothes. Yaashika took him to one that Semmi had contacts with. They both selected a few suits and outfits with slacks and shirts for a casual look also.

With shoes and socks and ties the total bill came out to just over fifteen thousand dollars. Yaashika took out a credit card and Semmi was only billed five thousand dollars.

"How come" Juan asked Yaashika, "that ten thousand dollars was taken off the bill?"

"The owner" she explained, "is a personal favorite of Semmi's and he gets special rates for his clients. Plus he also gets to date Semmi when she feels like it. Not too many men get to her anymore."

"Oh, I understand" Juan uttered.

When the clothes were packed they took the bags and waited outside for a minute or so while Min-jun drove up to the store and helped them into the SUV with their packages.

On the way back to Juan's apartment Yaashika explained to Juan that he now had to work and be straight with Semmi. He couldn't screw her on monies or he would be sorry. She did not have to elaborate; when Juan looked at the scar on Min-jun's face he knew he had to be careful and not screw her in anyway.

Min-jun pulled up to his building and was able to park in front. They all got out and each took a handful of bags and hangers and they walked to the elevator and then into Juan's apartment.

Once inside they helped him sort the clothes out and put everything away. Min-jun said he will be downstairs waiting and he left Juan and Yaashika alone.

"Okay" Yaashika to Juan, "let's see how you look so I can report back to Semmi.

"I don't understand" he said.

"I have to take pictures of you without clothes on, for our files. We need something to show select clients besides dress shots of you" she told him sweetly.

As she stood there watching, he took off his shirt and then his pants, until he was standing there completely naked for her inspection.

Yaashika took out her cell phone and started to take pictures of him. She explained that she needed him excited also, for a few shots. So she kneeled down and took him members and started to suck and lick it until he was aroused. She backed up a little and took the shots she needed.

Then she said it was time to try him out, and she undressed, and they both went to lie down on his bed.

Her dark breasts were firm and he handled them with caressing movements, playing with her and kissing her neck.

Slowly he moved down to below the pubic hair and started to lick and suck on her clitoris. She started to move and after a minute or so of gentle moaning she climaxed.

He had trouble holding on to her as she was moving very rapidly. Finally he pulled a pillow out from under her head and folded it and stuck it under her ass to elevate her. Then he entered her thrusting rapidly as he went in.

When they were finished Yaashika told him he did okay. She said she would recommend him to Brianna Jacobs so she could send him out on calls.

So now he was a male escort that Semmi could send out to both women and men. He was a valuable asset to her now.

Juan never asked how much he would be getting paid. He felt he didn't have to.

Yaashika left him five hundred dollars for an advance to buy food, and she got the address of his landlord. Min-jun drove her to the landlord and she went into see him. But it was an older woman, not a man.

"Hi, my names Yaashika and I'm here to pay the rent for Juan. He lives in the building you own in Chelsea."

"I'm glad some ones paying it. That building is the only one I own outright without partners. My husband died and we owned it together. The rest of our holdings are with partners who are royal pains in the ass" she told her in a grumpy tone of voice.

Yaashika continued speaking "Can I prepay for six months' rent for him, plus his back rent, in cash?" she asked knowing full well the answer.

The landlords tone changed immediately.

"Of course you can Sweetie. Wait a minute and I'll give you a receipt" she told her.

After she left the landlord's office Yaashika called Semmi and told her that the landlord might want to change her partnerships in the buildings she co-owned. It could be a good investment for her.

Chapter Fourteen - Follow up - Shaniqua

Shaniqua felt that if she went back to work as soon as possible it might help her mentally keep her mind off her loss.

The limo dropped her off at her apartment and as she unlocked the door the loneliness of the moment hit her. She stood at the threshold looking in at an empty home with no one there to greet her.

Instantly she missed her mother's voice welcoming her home. Then the loss of Eric came hurtling back at her as she gently rubbed her pregnant belly. The overwhelming feeling was setting back in and she knew she could not stay in this place tonight.

She stepped back outside into the hallway and took her cell phone out of her pocket. Shaniqua called the hotel she worked at and asked for the general manager. When he answered, knowing who she was and what she had asked, he immediately told her to come down and stay the night in one of their rooms.

Shaniqua hurriedly went back inside to her room and packed an overnight bag, and then walked quickly to the front door. She stepped outside then turned around, locked the door, and walked to the subway station around the corner to go to the hotel for the night.

The subway car was almost packed full of people sitting and standing, yet she felt alone in it. She had never had this feeling before but she was experiencing it now.

When she arrived in Times Square and walked up to the street level as she had done hundreds of times before she noticed, for the first time, how many people were walking around holding hands.

They were together and she was alone in a crowd of thousands. The impact was bearing down on her mentally and she hurried to the hotel entrance where she was greeted by the doorman and concierge as she entered the main lobby.

Alice was at the front desk and she smiled and greeted Shaniqua warmly and was genuinely glad to see her. After the many years of working together she felt empathy for her. Tears started to well up in both of their eyes and Alice told her how sorry she was to hear of her loss of Eric.

The general manager came out from the rear office and walked up to Shaniqua and expressed how sorry he was to hear of her loss. He turned to Alice and asked her to give Shaniqua the key to the large suite.

She thanked him and took the key and slowly went to the elevators to go upstairs to the room. Looking down at the key she realized that the room was the one they reserved for special guests and was not usually rented out to the public. It was the same one she used to take Eric to when they were together when he came into town for a day on business.

When the elevator door opened she walked out and turned to the left. It was the same path she took with Eric.

The walls seemed to close in on her as she made the turns in the hallway, going to the room at the end of the building. It was positioned there to be away from the elevators and give more quiet space to the special guests that stayed there.

When she put the plastic card key into the slot and opened the door happy memories came flooding back. But they made her sad.

As the tears started to roll down her cheek she looked at the empty bed and remembers Eric and her laying there in each other's arms. Kissing and embracing as lovers do.

As Shaniqua went to the window to look out she pulled the desk chair with her and placed it at the edge of the wall. She stared down at the masses moving below as one in Times Square as if in a trance. She was full of emotions yet her heart was empty and yearning for her lost fiancé. The love of her life, that she could not hold in her arms any more, was gone forever.

At the moment of her deepest despair her cell phone rang and she awoke form her daze to answer it.

"Hi Shaniqua, this is Ginger. Carl and I have been trying to call you for the last week but your phone must have been turned off."

"Oh, yes...it was. I'm sorry about that" Shaniqua answered.

She did not tell her that she was in a mental institution due to depression.

"Carl and I" Ginger continued, Carl and I were talking it over and we would like you to come live with us and have the baby here. Eric was our only child and we would very much like to have you in our family with your baby, and our only grandchild."

Shaniqua was silent for a moment. She did not expect this offer from them. Although she was in love with Eric she never had any other relationship with white people before, other than business.

But she remembers his parents warmly greeting her when she first met them with Eric and she was totally okay with what Ginger offered her.

"Yes" she answered. "I would love to come live with both of you. But I do have to work, I don't want to be a burden to anyone" she answered.

"I understand" Ginger said. "When you feel you are ready to work we will support you fully. Until then you can live with us, and even after the baby is born we want you to remain with us. You will be our daughter and I can't wait to hold my grandbaby. We will both be here for you."

Feeling better Shaniqua said good bye and started to plan her move to Maryland.

Chapter Fifteen - Follow up - Amanda

With the male nurse's phone number in her hand she got out of the limo and went upstairs to her apartment to call him.

The past week at the institute did not help her because she was mandated to be there by the court. It was not that she wanted to be there, she had to be there or go to jail. All Amanda did was follow their routine and answer whatever questions she was asked.

She unlocked her door and walked in to her living room and threw her coat down on the floor. She took out her cell phone and dialed a number. Amanda was going to call the male nurse from the institute when her phone rang in her hand.

It was him calling her to make a date.

He asked if she was free that evening and she answered yes, what did he have in mind.

They made arrangements for him to pick her up at her place and go out for dinner at a local bar he knew of.

So she put her clothes away that she had taken with her to the institute and began looking in her closet for an outfit to wear that evening.

Amanda selected a tight fitting white blouse with a very thin nude colored mesh sports bra to wear underneath it. Of course her form fitting black spandex jeans and black knee high boots were also taken out and placed near her bed. She never wore underwear, just a very small thong that didn't show panty lines.

She undressed and threw her clothes on her bed and then walked into the bathroom to start the shower running, trying to adjust it to her liking.

After her relaxing shower she was going to hang around the apartment and kill some time until she was ready to get dressed.

The hot water streamed down her body as she closed her eyes and stood there, enjoying the feeling of freedom.

Finally she turned off the water and stepped out onto a large beach towel that was on the floor so she wouldn't slip on the wet tiles. Carefully she reached for the soft designer bath towel hanging on the hook on the back of the bathroom door.

She had bought it online from a designer web site and it was extremely plush and absorbed a lot of moisture very quickly.

As Amanda was drying herself off she started to enjoy the softness of her new towel as she patted her lower abdomen. Gently she started to rub her inner thighs with it, feeling a slight rush going through her body.

She slowly slid down onto the beach towel that was on the floor. With her left hand Amanda started to rub herself almost to an orgasm. Just before she reached the zenith of her excitement she backed off, leaving an edge to her desires. She hoped that it would help when she met her date later that evening and they had sexual intercourse.

Finally she stood up and walked naked into her bedroom to start to get dressed for her date.

After doing her makeup and hair she was ready to have a good time and she could hardly wait for her front doorbell to ring.

Finally her date arrived and the bell rang twice. She walked briskly to the door to open it and greet him with anticipation of a great night out.

"Hi, come on in" she said to him.

"Thanks. This is a nice apartment you have here" he said as he entered the living room.

"Thank you. This was my grandmother's place but she had to move out due to illness" Amanda told him.

As she stood there with her full breasts bursting out of her white blouse he couldn't take his eyes off of her.

Finally he said to her "Amanda, you look great. But I feel there is a sexual tension between us. What if we have sex now; then we can go out together later tonight feeling much more relaxed with each other."

She still had her sexual edge on and she told him "Okay, come on into my bedroom with me."

He followed her in and as they were walking he started to take his shirt off and he kicked his shoes off also.

Standing in front of her bed they embraced and kissed wrapping their arms around each other tightly.

Amanda started to grind her body into his and she could feel him start to get aroused.

She stepped backwards and sat down on the bed and took her boots off. He leaned over to her and took hold of her hands and gently pulled her upright. Once she was standing he slid his hands around her waist and into the sides of her spandex jeans.

With one swift motion he started to slide them down towards the floor while she stepped out of them. As she stood there with no pants on he knelt down and started to kiss and lick her inner thighs. Slowly his tongue found its goal and she started to gyrate her hips slowly in an up and down motion.

As she was starting to reach an orgasm Amanda put her hands on the back of his head and pulled his face between her muscular legs. A long low moan came from deep inside of her as he continued what he was doing while taking his finger and inserting it in her.

As her legs were starting to give out from standing she turned sideways and bounced onto her bed; spreading her legs wide apart welcoming him to attend to her as she landed on the sheets.

He knelt on the bed between her legs and grabbing them under the knees he lifted them into the air as he entered her. Thrusting forcefully they both climaxed together and then collapsed into each other's arms. Kissing and gently biting each other on the neck they then embraced and just laid there together, intertwined on the bed.

As they were laying there Amanda's stomach began to feel hungry so she suggested that they get dressed and go out for dinner. She had her orgasm and he his, so they both were satisfied.

She said she knew of a very good sushi place only three blocks away. And they also had a liquor license and made great cocktails too.

He agreed and they both got dressed and as she said she had to go to the bathroom, he suggested that he get his car and pick her up by the front door.

Amanda said she would meet him at the curb and walked to her bathroom to clean up a bit and refresh her makeup.

As she turned on the light switch the small color balanced bulbs on each side of the mirror went on. She leaned in and opened her makeup pouch and took out her lipstick and a small compact.

When she was finished she turned off the lights and she left the apartment, locked her three locks, and walked downstairs to the sidewalk to wait for him.

She went to the curb and stood silently between two parked cars, expecting him to come around the corner any minute to pick her up.

But he never came.

Finally after thirty minutes she realized that he left and was not coming back for her.

She felt used and was very upset over this.

The only person she knew she could call and that would have a car pick her up was Bruce Donnelly, Juanita's ex-husband ad her sometime lover.

She was desperate and hungry and wanted to be taken care of. And she knew Bruce was the only one who could do that for her.

Amanda had left him before but they did continue to date. She had no feelings for him, the sex was so so, but the jewelry and the fact he wanted her was just now being realized by her. Being wanted was the key driver this time and she decided if he would take her back, she would stay with him.

"Hello Bruce, this is Amanda. What are you doing tonight? She asked him on her cell phone.

"Nothing very important Amanda" he answered her. "Would you like to come up and stay a while with me? I can send my driver to pick you up. Where are you now?" he asked her. Bruce knew the score and he was excited to be with her again. He knew she was slightly screwy but he was crazy about her, and why not?

She was decades younger, shapely, and very pretty. He was not interested in her intellect as he knew it was limited. But to him the sex was great; and she was eye candy when he took her out.

"I'm standing in front of my place. I'd really like to sec you again" she told him.

"Okay. I'm sending Leon to get you. Give him about thirty minutes or so" he told her.

When the black stretch limo drove up he double parked, got out to open the rear door for her, then once she was inside she sat back on the soft leather seats and relaxed. Putting her head back she closed her eyes and took a quick cat nap while the car drove slowly through Manhattan's bumper to bumper traffic.

When Leon finally arrived at Bruce's apartment the doormen were expecting her. They all remembered her name and called upstairs to inform Bruce that she was in the private elevator.

When Bruce opened the front door to his condo he smiled and greeted Amanda with a kiss. She put her arms around his neck and slowly and gently kissed him with her tongue rolling around inside his mouth, tenderly biting his lower lip.

He reached around her and with one arm pushed the door closed as he pulled her into the apartment.

She walked in and continued to kiss him passionately, rubbing her taught body against his until she felt him get aroused. She knew what he wanted and she was willing to let him play with her as long as he wanted. Finally she felt truly wanted.

But Bruce pulled back and took her by her hands and said he can't continue on like this.

"I miss you Amanda and I want you to move in full time with me. Your my baby doll and I need you with me."

He continued "I know there is a big age difference between us but we can overcome it. Please stay here with me forever" he asked her.

Amanda was desperate for love.

"Yes, Bruce. I will."

Chapter Sixteen - Follow up - Barbara

Finally back in her apartment Barbara decided to take another day or two off from work and rest.

Her girlfriend had an extra set of keys and went to the impound lot and drove her car back for her while she was away.

As she wriggled out of the limo she thanked the driver and walked slowly to her front door, passing her car in front of her garage.

She opened her mail box on the side of the entry and took out a few letters and stuffed them in her pocket as she unlocked her door to enter.

The light switch was on her left and the coat closet on the right as she slipped off her shoes and headed for her sofa to relax in.

As she sat down the mail in her pocket scratched her sides so Barbara shifted her body to the left and took out the letters to see what was there.

There were some bills and a letter hand addressed to her. It was from Brazil and the stamp on it was very pretty she thought.

But who in Brazil knew her, she thought to herself.

There was no return address and the mystery deepened for her.

Carefully she tore the envelope open and took out a two page letter that was addressed to her.

It was from John, her Master.

He wrote that he had been working as a computer consultant for a very large Wall Street bank for almost two years.

It was only in the last six months that he discovered a flaw in their security protocols and he had decided to breech their firewalls and get into their accounts.

Slowly over the last few months he had been transferring millions and millions of dollars to different off shore banks in various bank accounts that he owned.

But one day he heard the top executives speaking very excitedly about the missing money after a semi-annual audit and they were going to call in the Secret Service to investigate.

He knew they would find out where the funds went so he had to go personally and close out the accounts. He transferred most of the money to his Brazilian bank accounts and then went to St. Thomas and bought loose diamonds with his remaining money and swallowed them.

Being they were not metal he could pass through the metal detectors that the TSA had in the airport.

He took a taxi to the St. Thomas airport and boarded a flight to Mexico where he then transferred to another plane going to Brazil.

He wrote that he loved her and wanted her to come to Brazil to be with him. He said he would take care of all the travel arrangements.

Barbara had tears running down her cheeks as she read the letter.

She felt that he really did care for her and on the second page he wrote that he would be sending a ticket for her to fly down there to be with him.

The fact that it was stolen money did not faze her she was so excited to finally hear that he loved her. She really had no morality regarding this. The fact that he wrote her and wanted her was all she needed to know.

She struggled to get up and went over to her desk to turn on her computer. She wanted to see what the weather was in Brazil so she could pack accordingly.

When she was finished she turned it off and went over to her bed and started to get into her nightgown.

The excitement was wearing on her and she sat down on the side of the bed to catch her breath. Her heart was racing from excitement, she was extremely thrilled to be with her master again, and the adrenalin was pumping fast and furiously.

Barbara started to wheeze as she gasped for air. She tried to get air into her lungs when a sharp pain stung her in chest.

She had read that this was the start of a heart attack. Panicking she reached for her phone and dialed 911.

The operator answered but Barbara could not speak. She dropped the phone to the floor and collapsed on top of it.

The emergency operator heard the thud as Barbara fell and she kept asking if she was okay; but at the same time she sent the emergency services ambulance to Barbara's home as a safety precaution since there was no response.

When the ambulance arrived minutes later the front door was locked. One of them walked around to the side of the house and saw Barbara lying on the floor, spread eagled out on it.

He ran back around to the front of the house and they broke in the door and rushed to her bedroom to try to resuscitate her.

But it was too late, she was already blue.

They tried for fifteen minutes but couldn't get her breathing again.

Slowly they packed up their gear and called in the coroner's office to get the body.

They left and a policeman who arrived stayed there until the van came to take her away.

When the coroner finally came and was carting he rout of the house a postal truck arrived with an overnight package.

It was from Brazil and contained a direct flight ticket to Sao Paulo.

The End

37306251R00126

Made in the USA
Charleston, SC
04 January 2015